MISTRESS OF HER FATE

Lady Jane Holdenate, only child of Sir George Holdenate, is betrothed to the obnoxious Sir Edward Sutton, but the alliance is repugnant to Jane who is in love with the penniless John Fornton. In a fit of jealous rage, Sir Edward almost kills John in a duel. As he recovers, the lovers realise the only way to stop the wedding is to prove that Sir Edward is as wicked as his reputation, a task which uncovers danger, unsavoury situations and tests their love to the full.

JILL ARMITAGE

◆

MISTRESS OF HER FATE

Complete and Unabridged

LINFORD
Leicester

First published in Great Britain in 1999

First Linford Edition
published 2004

British Library CIP Data

Armitage, Jill
   Mistress of her fate.—Large print ed.—
Linford romance library
   1. Love stories
   2. Large type books
   I. Title
   823.9'14 [F]

   ISBN 1–84395–208–4

Published by
F. A. Thorpe (Publishing)
Anstey, Leicestershire

Set by Words & Graphics Ltd.
Anstey, Leicestershire
Printed and bound in Great Britain by
T. J. International Ltd., Padstow, Cornwall

This book is printed on acid-free paper

1

'Don't say another word, Sir Edward,' Jane commanded, her voice sounding strident and unnatural in her attempt to keep control. 'I don't know you, I don't love you and I certainly have no intentions of marrying you.'

'What has love got to do with it?' he asked impatiently, thumping his muscular thigh in an attempt to vent his frustration before he did so on this annoyingly stupid creature standing in front of him. 'Who said anything about love? Love is not important. This marriage is a business arrangement. It is your father's wish that I should wed you in order to avoid his estates falling into wardship.'

Sir Edward Sutton hunched his powerful shoulders and looked extremely pleased with himself.

'You are in a very vulnerable position, an underage, only child and a girl at that, with an ageing parent! You wouldn't stand a chance if anything happened to your father. You'd be made a ward of court and your lands taken by the state.'

'Sir, as heiress of Ladsill Hall, I have no intention of letting anyone take away what is rightfully mine,' Jane stated proudly.

Her angry face was still incredibly beautiful despite the lines of frustration creasing her brow.

'You come here telling me that I am to be your wife or I'll lose my inheritance. Never! I repeat, I have no wish to marry you and, as I see no reason for this discussion to continue, I wish you to leave, Sir Edward.'

'Whether you like it or not, you, my dear, will become my wife. It was either that or you could be my ward.'

He laughed sardonically, a nasty smile creasing his florid, flabby features and his eyes held a mockery that she ached to wipe away with a resounding smack.

'If I became your guardian I would get all these lands and the right to sell you in marriage to the highest bidder, so I rather think the idea of marriage to me has more appeal. I assure you my interest will not be purely avuncular.'

Sir Edward's voice droned dangerously as he reached over and ran his finger slowly, menacingly, down her upper arm in a flagrant gesture of intimacy. With one swift, defiant jerk, she threw her arm backward to dislodge his finger. His hand remained suspended for a long second before he dropped it resignedly to his side. He made no further move.

'Well, well, I seem to have got myself a sporty little wench. Taming you will be a pleasure, my pretty one.'

He let out a harsh, throaty laugh and a waft of foul breath fanned Jane's face.

'If my father was here, you would not make such a statement. I beg you, my lord, I have been extremely civil and although you have provoked me, I am willing to accept your apology and forget this conversation ever happened.'

'Apology! Why should I apologise? Do I, for some reason, owe you an apology, my lady?'

He shifted his enormous frame, further emphasised by the bulk of his square-shouldered jacket, and stood hands on hips and legs apart in an attempt to mirror a powerful stance. His grey trunk hose, pumpkin shaped and bombasted with padding, were worn over full stockings that pulled tightly, emphasising the stout contours of his short, muscular legs.

'I hardly think you can fail to see my displeasure, Sir Edward,' she said coolly although her cheeks were flushed and her eyes bright with anger.

'It's time you had a man to wed you, my lady.'

'How dare you, sir! You are so maddeningly persistent.'

She shied away from him like a petrified horse, turning away to grip the stone rail of the balustrading. She felt trapped, not just physically, between the

4

stout stone balustrade and the bulky frame of Sir Edward Sutton, but mentally, by filial duties. Why hadn't her father told her of this arrangement with Sir Edward? She felt dizzy and slightly sick as she tried to block out the unfathomable words that still buzzed in her ears. To think that the honour of the house of Holdenate should end like this. She, the daughter of that house, had changed hands like a piece of valueless merchandise and now instead of being her father's property, she would soon belong to this man standing behind her puffing himself up with egotistical arrogance.

Her eyes darted wildly around as if searching for an escape in the serene country garden. Unshed tears stung her eyes and she blinked heavy lids, temporarily closing out the spectacular views where the Ladsill pleasure grounds merged into wooded country-side and a panorama of hills beyond. Leaning heavily against the stone balustrading, she gripped the stone rail with such determination, the rough surface digging painfully into her smooth, gloveless hands. She felt his eyes boring into her. Barely controlled panic kept her back turned to him.

Sir Edward scrutinised the slight frame clinched into an impossibly tiny waist. He calculated that he could span that petite waist with his strong hands. He should grab her by the shoulders, drag her round forcibly to face him and pin her against the balustrading where she would be powerless, and seal their betrothal with a kiss. Yet he drew back. Something about the determined set of her slight shoulders unnerved him. But Lady Jane, willing or not, would give herself to him. He could wait.

All this will soon be mine, Sir Edward thought smugly, looking up at the mullion-windowed mansion with its broken lines framed in clustering ivy and letting his gaze travel over the closely-shaven, emerald lawn which extended along the length of the crenellated, pale stone front. Several peacocks strutted about the lawn.

He turned away, almost stepping on two sleeping spaniels that lay at the feet of their mistress. He couldn't help thinking what stupid, worthless animals they were. Give him a pair of hounds or a good gun-dog any day. Real dogs, man's dogs, working dogs, useful dogs, not these powdered, pampered pets.

An old crone hobbled towards them.

'Good-day sir,' she offered, dipping a slight curtsey then turned her attention to Jane who turned slowly, reluctantly, her gaze falling explosively on Sir Edward who still stood, eyeing her with lustful interest.

'I was thinking what a perfect day it is.' Old Bess smiled. 'Yet your face belies the fact, my lady.'

Jane pointed a weak smile in Bess's direction yet the smile froze on her face as she turned towards Sir Edward.

'There is no reason to delay your departure, my lord. My nurse will escort you to the courtyard.'

'Aye, my lady, but your father is just

arriving and I think he may wish to see Sir Edward,' Bess stated hastily, studying Jane's unhappy face. 'Is there aught amiss, my little one?'

'Nothing that can't be put right now my father is home, Bess,' she acknowledged, turning towards the terrace steps where Sir George Holdenate stood momentarily surveying the scene.

He was a very patrician-looking gentleman, robust and hale, with thick, wavy greying hair. With a look of determination painted on his stern countenance, he descended the steps and strode towards the assembled group.

'My lord father,' Jane muttered bowing her head in greeting.

Sir George Holdenate gave a slight inclination of his head to Sir Edward before turning to Jane and offering her a heavily-ringed hand.

'Come walk with me, Jane. If you will excuse, Sir Edward.'

It wasn't a question so much as a statement as father and daughter moved away slowly.

'I assume Sir Edward has proposed marriage to you just now,' he began looking directly ahead.

'He has, Father, yet I find it hard to believe that you have failed to mention any of this to me prior to his visit. According to Sir Edward, the decision has already been made between you and him. At no time have my wishes been taken into consideration. Couldn't we have discussed this?'

'There was no need. You are not the only person involved in the decision. Hasn't it occurred to you what this alliance will mean to our future security? If I died tomorrow, what would become of you and Ladsill?'

He paused, giving Jane a quick glance but her eyes were downcast.

'I have taken the only course open to us to protect your inheritance. I want to be sure you are looked after and all my estates are safely passed on to your children.'

'Better for me to die tomorrow than

be forced to marry against my will. How could life be bearable with a man I don't love?'

'Love? That will come later. Respect is more important at this stage. Sir Edward can offer you security and position. He has land and connections.'

'We have land and connections, Father, and you have offered all of this to Sir Edward as well as myself. I am to be handed over just like another possession.'

'Don't talk such nonsense. You need a man to take care of you.'

'I don't need a man for anything, especially not that man.'

'You are wrong, Jane.'

Sir George gave a deep sigh and shook his head slowly as they paused under the welcome shade of a gnarled, old tree that offered an exceptional vantage point over the grounds of Ladsill Hall, the perfect picture of an English country house set like a jewel in a casket of tranquil English countryside. Jane sat down slowly on the bench seat but Sir George paced up and down for a few minutes in agitation. Eventually he paused and looked around him.

'This land is held by knight service. In early feudal times, the Crown gave land in exchange for a knight or two to enable an army to be raised quickly and cheaply.'

Jane's voice mirrored her vexation.

'Don't play me for a fool, Father. My knowledge may be limited but even I know that practice has now ceased.'

'The custom may have lapsed, but the Crown is determined to keep its rights by strengthening its claims. When lands are inherited by an under-age child, the knight service can't be performed, so with perfect logic, the Crown takes back its land in lieu of service until the heir is old enough. In order to avoid this, I was arranging for all my lands to be given to trustees, then Sir Edward made me an offer I couldn't refuse.'

'However good the offer, I would have refused it,' Jane argued, flashing him a defiant look.

'I know that and Sir Edward knows that, too. That's why we conducted all the negotiations without your knowledge. All right, perhaps I didn't do the right thing. Perhaps I should have informed you then waited for a month or two, given you time to get to know Sir Edward. Would that have helped? If we delay announcing your betrothal will you change your mind?'

'Never.'

'Just as I thought!'

'Please let me go to my room, Father.'

'No. Trust me, Jane, I know what is best for you. I've watched you grow into a fine, young woman and I've watched the interest in the eyes of many young swains who would like to get close to you. But you would have none of them and it is your perverseness that has both helped and hindered my decision. I could never offer you to someone who could not match you in intelligence or spirit but I think Sir

Edward can and now my mind is made up. The sooner you are betrothed the better.'

As he spoke, he steered her back to where Sir Edward and Bess watched and waited.

'Take my hand, Jane,' Sir George ordered in firm tones.

Slowly, she placed her trembling fingers in his, lowered her eyes and waited expectantly. In the silence that followed, Sir George ceremonially placed Jane's small hand in the clammy palm of Sir Edward Sutton. She wanted to pull away. His hand was dirty, yet she remained rigid and unfeeling, desperately trying to close her mind to Sir Edward's touch.

'I have today pledged my daughter to Sir Edward Sutton,' Sir George stated in a tone as impersonal and business like as if he were discussing disposing of his wheat or horse or any other possession.

Old Bess let out an audible gasp of disbelief as she lowered her ample frame on to a seat to stop the garden spinning, taking Sir George's words with it.

'You, Jane, will become the wife of Sir Edward,' Sir George continued, 'and I give you both my blessing.'

A look of satisfaction spread over Sir Edward's podgy face as with over exaggerated solemnity, he remarked, 'May the union of my house and the house of Holdenate be knit in a bond of undying friendship.'

'Amen to that,' Sir George agreed thoughtfully eyeing his daughter with a certain amount of disappointed apprehension.

He could not understand her reluctance. What could be wrong with the girl? Didn't she understand the situation at all?

'If I may venture to say,' Sir Edward continued, not allowing his panache to get dented, 'this union will be a good one for both families.'

'It will certainly be a memorable one,' Sir George said with a wry smile.

'For you, my child, I'll make sure that the wedding surpasses anything this county has ever seen.'

'Thank you, Father,' she said dutifully, flashing a stony glare at Sir Edward as he reached forward to draw her arm through his.

'If you will excuse me,' Jane stated firmly, snatching her arm away from Sir Edward's touch, 'this has been quite a surprise and Bess and I have things to discuss.'

She threw a quick look at the silent Bess whose lined face now looked solemn and unreadable.

'Wait, my dear. I thought tonight we would celebrate your betrothal,' Sir George stated. 'This is an auspicious day and surely that gives us cause for rejoicing.'

'Yes, Father, if you say so, although I fail to see why the announcement of my betrothal should justify this feverish haste. Can we wait a month or two until a suitable celebratory feast can be arranged? Perhaps Christmas or the spring. Yes, in the spring, travel would be better then.'

Sir George read his daughter's expression and shook his head.

'No. Plans are already in operation for this evening. The head steward has been informed and all the pages that can be spared are riding round the district with the news and invitations to everyone who would like to come to feast with us tonight. All will be welcome.'

Jane bowed her head in disappointment. Everything had been arranged, even the evening's festivities where there would be plenty of drunken revelry and little ceremony. A sob tore her throat as Jane resigned herself to the knowledge that her father was taking Sir Edward's offer against her will and soon everyone would know that she was the bride elect of Sir Edward Sutton. She was just a pawn in the game, to be moved at will.

Bess jerked her head and snorted her own disapproval, sending her snowy white cap awry as they made their curtsies and turned to walk slowly away along the terrace. The two dogs ran ahead playfully, returning at intervals to check on their young mistress and her ageing nurse who sauntered along at a leisurely pace.

'That's a pretty turn up for the books,' Bess stated as soon as they were out of earshot of the two men. 'Gave me quite a turn, that did. What a shock! Such a surprise!'

'If you were surprised, think how I felt! Sir Edward Sutton is a stranger to me. He has paid me no attention, then suddenly a few hours ago he sprang this ridiculous suggestion on me and told me it was all arranged.'

Jane turned to Bess, her eyes full of anguish and wretchedness, her voice as shaky as her legs.

'I thought my father would dismiss the whole thing as a practical joke and send Sir Edward on his way but he didn't. He confirmed what Sir Edward had said and more. Oh, Bess, this is the

17

worst day of my life.'

'There, there, my pet.'

Bess took Jane's hand reassuringly and steered her towards a favourite seat surrounded by the exhilarating fragrance of lavender bushes.

'Your father must have given the matter some serious consideration if he wants you to accept the attentions of Sir Edward Sutton. Do you think you could grow to like Sir Edward?'

'How can you ask such a question, Bess? I had never said more than two words to him before today but now after our conversation, I hate him. Everything about him is distasteful to me. Just look at him! He's grotesque. If my father forces me into this marriage, my life will be one long penance.'

'Nay, child, don't upset yourself so. He's no handsome gallant I must admit, but he must have other assets to compensate him for his lack of good looks.'

'Like what?' Jane asked. 'Tell me one good thing about him!'

'I don't know Sir Edward, but his father was a good man. The family has great estates in Yorkshire and Lancashire.'

'So you think I should accept his offer because he's titled and wealthy?'

'No, my pet. Those would not be my sole priorities, but no shortage of material things certainly makes life easier. You don't know what it's like to be poor. My parents had ten of us and we all lived in a room no bigger than your chamber. There was never enough to eat particularly in the winter, and the cold! Even wearing everything we owned we were still cold and . . . '

'Yes, Bess, yes,' Jane interrupted. 'I've heard this story so many times and it doesn't change.'

She quirked an eyebrow expressively.

'No, my pet, but what I'm saying is, you can't marry outside your class. It's just not done. You're a lady and Sir Edward is a gentleman, in title at least, and you are of the same faith. Isn't that enough to be going on with?'

As she spoke, Bess looked at Jane steadily, noting the preoccupied expression and the angry flush that was disappearing from her cheeks.

'Can you think of nothing in his favour?'

Jane smirked, then leaned over conspiratorially.

'I think he has a striking resemblance to our Queen's father, the late King Henry, with his florid face and unwieldy appearance, and I think he deliberately dresses in the same fashion, wearing outmoded styles in colours as dark and dull as he is, in order to foster the resemblance.'

Jane stopped exasperatedly as Bess smiled and shook her head sagely.

'I don't think your father has given this choice a lot of thought, but his reasons are sound.'

'Sound,' Jane echoed. 'Would it be any worse to be made a ward or to be made to wed?'

'Nay, my pet, you have so much to learn. You are so young and beautiful and so vulnerable. A suitable suitor must be selected by parents. It's a great pity that your dear mother died before making a choice. She would have known whom to choose and how to convince your father that he was the right choice. Sir George loved your mother dearly and her untimely death has obviously made him aware that his may be soon. Then what will happen to you, my little one? You need a husband. A woman of your station must marry.'

'But why Sir Edward?' Jane asked pensively, pulling at a stem of lavender and sniffing as the scented heads popped off.

'Because your father and Sir Edward's father were great friends before his tragic death. He was a good Catholic who stood by his religious convictions even at the cost of his life. If his son is half the man his father was, your father's choice is a good one. You don't know Sir Edward yet, but the wedding will not be for many months so you will have the chance of

21

getting to know him before then. You might even get to like him.'

Jane let out a soft moan and Bess gave her hand a gentle, reassuring squeeze. They sat for a long time in uneasy silence. Jane's head was bowed as she stared blindly down at the wide square toes of her shoes that peeped out from below her heavy skirts.

'I'm not ripe for marriage, Bess,' Jane admitted at last, biting her lip and burning with confusion. 'I know nothing about the duties of a wife to her husband. I don't want a man to dominate me, to wield power over my body. I don't want to be compliant.'

Bess knew Jane's words were a cry for help as she bent her head to draw Jane's eyes to hers.

'All in good time, my pet,' she said placing her hand on Jane's reassuringly. 'You have a great capacity for loving although as yet Sir Edward has obviously been unable to arouse any such feelings. Just give yourself time.'

Bess's words were said with more

conviction than she felt. Unfortunately, she had seen the lecherous way Sir Edward looked at her innocent, young charge and doubted whether he would be content to give her time. She hated the thought of her pet being subject to the greedy, sexual appetite of such a man.

'Did you ever consider marriage, Bess?'

'Glory be.' Bess laughed, drawn gratefully out of her disturbing thoughts. 'Oh, I had my chances, but I also had my position here. I was your mother's tire woman and very proud and happy I was to be that. I couldn't have worked for a kinder, sweeter lady. When you were born, I was the first person to hold you. I heard your first cries and I knew then that my place was with you for as long as you needed me.'

'Oh, Bess, I will always need you,' Jane cried wrapping her arms round the old nurse. 'I will need you more than ever to help me through this time. How can I celebrate a betrothal that is so distasteful to me?'

Nurse Bess raised a questioning eyebrow as she studied Jane's perplexed face.

'By remembering you're a lady and whatever you might think or feel, you must never let your emotions show. Think only how fortunate you are, then be grateful.'

'I'll try to remember that but it won't be easy tonight, not in front of all those people.'

'Fiddle. The people who come tonight will be here to feast and make merry. They'll be understandably interested in you and Sir Edward for the first five minutes then they'll be too busy enjoying themselves. Believe me, after an hour, you could slip away and no-one would notice.'

'Oh, Bess, you are so funny. If only I could believe you. I might just be able to act the part of a nervous, bride-to-be for an hour. It's the long term that terrifies me.'

'I know, but just take it one step at a

time. I'm sure Sir Edward will be only too aware of your dislike for him and if he's any sense he'll withdraw before it's too late.'

'But, Bess, that would be dreadful,' Jane almost screamed. 'All the county would then know that he had passed me over, abandoned me, jilted me. I couldn't live with the shame.'

Bess was mortified. Her well-intentioned words had resounded so cruelly she wanted to tear out her tongue. Rather than helping the situation, the life-line she had thrown had been the final humiliation and Jane sobbed inconsolably in Bess's arms. As the sobs subsided, a young maid from the house approached hurriedly, her face wreathed in a happy smile.

'Lady Jane, your father sends word that you must start your preparations for this evening,' she said with a broad smile. 'Everyone is really busy and looking forward to tonight's celebrations.'

Reluctantly they returned to the house, the maid running on ahead while Bess encouraged Jane to show an outwardly happy face.

In the banqueting hall, fresh, sweet-smelling flowers from the garden were being strewn to give a festive touch to the clean scented rushes covering the stone slabs. They also served as floor seating if more people arrived than the benches could accommodate. The smell of myrrh was thick in the air as several housemaids rubbed the seeds of sweet fern into the furniture to bring out a glossy finish while others hauled on the thick ropes to hoist numerous candle brackets up into the beamed roof of the great hall.

The dais tables gleamed with silver plates and dishes and two jewelled salts. Below the dais, extra trestles, boards and benches were being placed down the length of the hall. These were laid with more gleaming plates and vessels. Everywhere the frenzied activity announced the drawing near of the evening activities and Jane felt even more miserable.

She looked around her with a mixture of interest and alarm before mounting the steep stone staircase to the upper landing. There amongst the wilderness of narrow corridors, she pushed open a roughly hewn door on the left, and pulling aside the tapestry, entered her own low-ceilinged chamber. Bess followed, perching herself on a stool by the fire from where she directed Jane's lavish preparation. With the help of her tire woman Jane was dressed in a trained velvet kirtle with sleeves tight to the elbow then turned back to form deep hanging cuffs lined with fur. Her contrasting under-sleeves were flashed and tied with ribbons.

On the four-poster bed lay an assortment of exotically shaped head-dresses. Jane eyed the assorted gable hoods in their rich fabrics trimmed with embroidery and jewels, and dismissed them all. From the horseshoe shape of the velvet French hoods she made a choice.

'I'll wear this, if you dress my hair to suit.'

Bess nodded her agreement and Jane's hair was tied into silk rolls and concealed under the hood.

2

A warm breeze like the breath of a furnace came toiling over the open Derbyshire countryside heralding the eve of another glorious autumn day. Many farm labourers headed to The Peacock, a coaching inn on the Ladsill estate, where they could indulge in gossip and the landlord's strong ale, preferably on the benches outside as few cared to sit inside the stuffy, ill ventilated rooms in such weather.

Mary Armstrong, the landlord's daughter, was busy with a spinning wheel as her tongue kept time to the whirr of the wheel, yet even she stopped and watched as the young page from Ladsill Hall dismounted and walked towards the assembled group.

'Greetings my friends,' he called before broadcasting the news of Lady

Jane's betrothal and passing out invitations to the evening's festivities.

With shouts of affirmation ringing in his ears, the page entered the hostelry where Hubert Armstrong poured him a jack of strong ale.

'You might as well close for the evening, landlord,' the page laughed accepting his drink. 'Everyone will be at Ladsill Hall tonight.'

'Aye, but what do I do wi' them?' Hubert Armstrong asked indicating through the open back doorway where two gentlemen played a game of bowls on the extensive green.

The young men's fashionable silhouettes from the broad shoulders of their short, flared capes to the soft leather shoes on their well-shaped legs spelled out gentry.

'Who are they?' the page asked Armstrong with interest.

'No idea,' the landlord answered. 'Gentlemen of quality though, by their dress. They rode in about two hours ago and stalled their horses before indulging in a game of bowls. They've got a valet each but they'll say nothing about their masters' business. I'd come up to the Hall and leave them with my Mary but she'll probably want to come, too.'

'I know, I'll invite these gentlemen to be my lord's guests, too,' the page suggested. 'Do you think they'll accept?'

'I warrant they will, unless they're graceless churls or pressed for time, which doesn't seem to be the case,' the landlord replied.

Closely followed by Hubert Armstrong, the page walked down the passage and out into the garden. He doffed his cap and addressed the two players who looked at him enquiringly.

'Sirs, I am a page in the service of Sir George Holdenate, Lord of Ladsill Hall,' he explained in a practised fashion. 'Tonight there will be a feast at the Hall in honour of the betrothal of Lady Jane, daughter of my lord. Everyone is welcome and if your circumstances allow you to attend, you will be sure of good hospitality.'

The two gentlemen smiled and looked at each other in bewilderment.

'But your lord doesn't know us, nor we him,' one exclaimed laughing. 'We are strangers to these parts and may well be scurvy knaves.'

'It doesn't matter, sir. The invitation still holds firm.'

'Then yes, we would be pleased to attend this feast, wouldn't we, Will?' the first gentleman replied, hugely delighted at the unceremonious form of invitation. 'I know of Sir George Holdenate's hospitality. Did you say the celebration is to mark the betrothal of his daughter?'

'That is my information, sir. Lady Jane is betrothed to Sir Edward Sutton,' the page answered.

'Tell me,' the first gentleman said, his interest fully aroused, 'is there any truth in the stories that Lady Jane's beauty is matchless?'

'Sir,' the page replied with a bow, 'I am a humble servant, but if you will accept me as a judge, I'd say that Lady Jane has no equal in England.'

'Come, come,' the second gentleman, previously referred to as Will, teased, 'that is a bold statement.'

'I would challenge any to say otherwise,' the page cried enthusiastically.

'Your sentiments do credit to you, good fellow. It's obvious Lady Jane doesn't lack a champion. Here's a groat for your staunchness.'

As he spoke, the gentleman threw a groat into the air and the amazed page caught it deftly.

'And this beautiful lady is betrothed to Sir Edward Sutton, you say?'

'Yes, sir. Do you know him?'

'I know of him, although I can think of nothing I've heard to his credit,' the gentleman said with a laugh.

'Watch your tongue, sir,' the landlord snapped, evidently annoyed. 'If you have heard rumours against Sir Edward you would be better not to repeat them as he's a good patron of mine. I can assure you that my Lord of Ladsill would not entertain Sir Edward if his record was not clean.'

'His record is clean because he is clever in deceit,' the gentleman replied.

Hubert Armstrong opened his mouth to continue but the second gentleman intervened.

'What does it matter anyway? We have no interest in these people or Sir Edward Sutton.'

'You are right, Will,' his friend agreed turning to the page.

'Make my obeisance to your lord and say that I, John Fornton, son of the Earl of Leyland, and my friend here, William Alleyne Esquire, will be honoured to partake of Ladsill's hospitality this evening.'

The page, who had been standing silently listening, now opened wide eyes as he learned the status of the speaker.

'I will give my lord your message, sir,' he replied with a small bow as he left the group.

Hubert Armstrong's hateful, hard

eyes had never left John Fornton's face as if he found him distasteful in some way. John, aware of his piercing gaze, made light of the situation by ordering more ale and with his command, Hubert Armstrong had no option but to turn and walk away in a grumpy, obsequious manner.

'We are in favour tonight, Will,' John said, slapping his friend on his heavily-padded shoulder. 'Gossips wax eloquent when they speak of the beauty of Sir George's daughter. I've heard her referred to as the belle of Ladsill, so tonight should be most interesting.'

'For you perhaps, my friend, but I had arranged other interests to occupy my time tonight. If you drag me off to Ladsill Hall you will be depriving me of the company of the most agreeable wench I've set eyes on for the last few days.'

'Sorry, old friend, but I would wager a bet that if it's Mary you are referring to, she'll be at Ladsill Hall tonight, too. She doesn't strike me as the kind of girl to pass up an invitation like that. Now, let's finish our game. After that we'll give some attention to our appearance, because tonight our quality warrants we'll be sitting above the salt.'

That evening, John and William, handsomely dressed and each wearing, on his hip, a sword and jewelled-handled rapier as their status entitled them to, rode slowly towards Ladsill Hall, entranced by its setting. They moved into single file to ride across the narrow, stone bridge spanning the river, and as they cleared it on the other side, the warder on watch in the Eagle Tower blew a warning blast on his horn. Instantly the lower gate was thrown open by the sentry. Two grooms came forward to take the horses and the Great Chamberlain stood in the archway to receive the strangers.

The two men made themselves known and were conducted by one of the chamberlain's stewards to Sir George Holdenate. He received them graciously, and when they attempted to offer something like an apology for what they considered their unceremonious intrusion, he set them at their ease at once.

'Gentlemen,' he said heartily, 'this is a memorable night in the history of Ladsill Hall, as it marks the betrothal of my daughter, Lady Jane, to Sir Edward Sutton. On such an occasion, churl indeed I would be to close my gate against anyone who claimed admission in the name of hospitality. I feel fortunate that chance should have given me the opportunity of welcoming you as honoured guests. What brings you gentlemen to this area?'

'This visit was totally unplanned, sir,' John replied. 'We should be in London but I was summoned from the capital by an urgent message that one of my kinsmen had been taken suddenly ill. I am pleased to say that the illness has proved more alarming than dangerous.'

'I am very pleased to hear it,' the gracious host said, 'but who, sir, are your kinsmen in this vicinity?'

'Lord and Lady Turbot of Migfield Manor,' John replied proudly. 'Gertrude Turbot is my sister.'

'My dear sir, that makes you doubly welcome this evening. Indeed, your sister was a good friend to my late wife. I hope that your sister and family are now well.'

'Indeed they are sir, thank you,' John replied.

The arrival of more guests of some consequence put an end to the interview and the two young men were left to their own devices. Presently, the heralds announced, by the blowing of trumpets, that the feast was spread. The inferior guests were already in their places, but those who were privileged to sit above the salt formed a line in the hall waiting for the newly-betrothed couple to enter to lead the way. John and William stood together as Lady Jane and Sir Edward entered and walked towards the dais.

'By God's truth, Will,' John whispered to his friend, 'for once the

38

rumours haven't lied. The daughter of the house is even fairer than reports have painted her.'

William's and John's eyes were both on Jane being escorted down the hall on the arm of her betrothed. Her pale skin had the opalescent bloom of beauty and from under drooping silken lashes and well-arched brows, eyes of the clearest emerald green sparkled like shards of glass. They were questioning eyes that searched the throng for a familiar face, yet John was amazed to see sorrow and even a hint of fear held in their depths. He suddenly had an unaccountable need to know why this beautiful creature should look so troubled on what should have been such a romantic occasion.

'Does Sir Edward Sutton remind you of King Henry?' William whispered with a slight mocking laugh and the corner of John's mouth dented slightly as he gave his friend a knowing look.

'I would rather look at Lady Jane than her betrothed,' John replied as the family group took their seats and the remaining guests were conducted by the chamberlain and his stewards to the upper table.

'Indeed, but remember that the lady is now spoken for, my friend. I don't want you to make an enemy of Sir Edward Sutton. I hear he's a fine swordsman.'

'Have no fear, Will, I will be most discreet,' John replied sitting down in the offered seat.

He looked round with satisfaction and was delighted to find himself seated opposite Jane, although several seats lower. His view of her was hardly obstructed, and he found it hard to refrain from staring almost rudely. Until that moment, she hadn't noticed him, then suddenly their eyes met for the first time. She dropped them immediately then half turned her head. After a brief spell, she glanced again and blushed crimson as she saw that he was still watching her.

John dipped his hands into the bowl

of rose water and wondered again what a lovely lady like Jane could see in Sir Edward Sutton who was making a great show of wrestling a peacock leg from its socket with belligerent determination. The guests at the high table were entertaining but John found it hard to concentrate on his neighbours' conversations as many times he looked furtively past them to glimpse Jane over his raised goblet.

Their eyes contacted again and John gave a slight inclination of his head in acknowledgement. She looked away and John sliced himself a piece of peacock which he impaled on the end of his dagger. As he began eating he glanced up and caught Jane watching him. Never before had looking been so electric as for a timeless moment their eyes held. He noted that she blushed most charmingly then she lowered her eyes and turned away.

Inwardly, Jane's emotions were by no means as under control as she made it seem. She had no appetite, for her eyes

41

failed to register any detail of the food before her. The guests at the high table were entertaining, but her ears strained to catch the sound of the stranger's voice above the volume of laughter and voices that seemed to be getting louder by the minute.

Sir Edward continued helping himself greedily to handfuls of food, some of which oozed out from between his chubby fingers. His movements had a barely-controlled violence about them as he gulped back his wine which ran in rivulets down his bearded chin. With a bang, he slammed down his goblet and pulled the length of his sleeve across a greasy, wet mouth.

'Why aren't you eating, woman?' he asked through a mouthful of chicken thigh.

Jane gave no answer as she prodded the meat on her plate disinterestedly, further disgusted as wafts of Sir Edward's foul breath fanned her face. Competing with the sound of the general revelry, the minstrels in the gallery sang and played serenades appropriate to the occasion as Sir George's guests proved to be very lively dinner companions. The explosions of riotous hilarity and noisy tongues gave evidence that the guests were falling under the influence of the host's strong ales and excellent wines.

Jane toyed with her food, wishing she could leave and seek the cool air of the evening but whenever she caught her father's eye and threw him a look of eloquent appeal, his instinctive aversion to his daughter's plight brought no sympathy. Only John Fornton's looks, wistfully caressing the contours of her unaware face, saw how gracefully this embodiment of womanly perfection conducted herself and he watched, entranced, waiting and hoping for a look or perhaps a smile. But Jane seemed unable to smile and John again had an unaccountable need to know why this celebration should bring her no pleasure.

Eventually the health and happiness

of the betrothed was proposed by one of the oldest tenants and duly honoured accompanied by plenty of shouting, uninhibited laughter and emphatic expressions of goodwill. The gimmal ring was broken into its three parts, to be reunited later as the wedding ring. One part was placed on Jane's finger, one for Sir Edward and the third given to Sir George as their witness. John studied Jane's perfect face earnestly, yet still she showed no sign of emotion.

Presently, a toast was proposed to the ladies who, shortly afterwards, departed from the hall, leaving the men to indulge more liberally in liquor. Sir George and many at the upper table rose at midnight to indulge in cards in a private back room, but the others showed no intention of leaving. The occasion was an exceptional one so the servants were instructed to place a fresh supply of liquor on the tables and not to begin to extinguish the candles before two o'clock.

As Sir George was about to leave the

banqueting hall, John and William followed and approached him to pay their respects and take their leave.

'No,' he exclaimed jovially, 'it's not fitting that you ride forth at such an hour. Chambers are at your disposal if you will accept the shelter of my house for the night.'

John expressed his thanks eagerly. This unexpected invitation to spend the night at Ladsill Hall would hopefully give him the opportunity of seeing Jane in the morning. Perhaps he might even get the chance to speak to her.

When John woke the following morning, the sunlight of a glorious autumn morning was streaming through the stone-mullioned window of his tapestried bedchamber. Surprised to hear the turret bell count out the hour of nine, he ashamedly swung himself up from the curtained bed, pulled on his outer garments and walked over to the silver bowl filled with rose-water to refresh himself. Having attended to his ablutions and dressed fully, he left the room to take some much needed fresh air.

As there was no sign of William, John requested a page to show him the way to the gardens where he found himself on the upper terrace, walking to and fro in a pensive mood thinking how he might get to see Lady Jane before he left. The rules of courtesy dictated that he could not prolong his stay for any length of time after breakfast. From the upper terrace a steep flight of steps led down into the principle garden and John descended the stone steps thoughtfully.

'Floretta, Felicity, stop. Come here, you disobedient dogs.'

A silvery voice fraught with frustration broke into his thoughts as two silky spaniels charged towards him. They obviously felt it their duty to gallop along the lawn, yelping and snapping and intent, it would seem, on making their teeth sink into the stranger's well-shaped calves. He stood unmoved, waiting for the appearance of the lady with the silvery voice. He was not disappointed to find that it was Jane. As she rounded the banks of rhododendrons, skirts held high to aid her run, she saw the stranger standing ahead of her and stopped abruptly. Her indignant gaze moved from John to the now placid animals, wagging their tales in welcome.

'I had no idea anyone was here,' she stammered, her face flushed with exertion, vexation and embarrassment.

Painfully aware that she did not present a very dignified picture, she ran her hand over her escaping locks, tried to straighten her tight-fitting bodice and leaned forward instinctively to smooth down her crumpled overskirts.

'My dogs are not in the habit of running away from me or attacking strangers,' she pointed out mildly, straightening up to face him, only to drop her eyes as she registered the blaze of interest in his bold stare.

'Indeed, Lady Jane, these ferocious animals fill me with such fear that I crave to place myself under your protection,' John answered with a bemused smile and feigned fright.

Jane looked up and smiled, something that John couldn't remember her doing at all the previous evening.

'It's strange that my dogs should have been so unmannerly. I've never known them to act like this before.'

She turned from John as Bess, who had obviously been walking in the gardens with her, joined them.

'My dogs are normally very well behaved, aren't they, Bess?'

'Aye, my lady, they are,' old Bess replied as she raised sceptical eyebrows and eyed the stranger with a combination of suspicion and approval. 'Maybe something in this handsome gallant's manners offended them, my lady.'

'Then I'm lucky as it's given me the opportunity to pay my respects to my host's charming daughter and offer you my felicitations on your betrothal.'

He doffed his plumed hat which almost touched the ground as he made a deep bow to the ladies. Without a hat, Jane recognised the stranger from last night's banquet and she felt the blush rush over her cheeks as she remembered the interest in those glittering eyes. Now she had a chance to see him entirely to complete her fragmented image of him from the previous evening and she was not disappointed.

'I would like to know the name of my father's guest who seems so well versed in flattery,' she said demurely, in a soft, musical voice.

'Lady Jane,' he answered softly, 'flattery to one as beautiful as yourself would be an impertinence.'

The smile accompanying the words lit his handsome features with irresistible charm and Jane was overcome by a physical awareness she had never experienced before. Sunlight was glinting on his raven black hair, highlighting the angular planes of his handsome face. This man was having a most disturbing effect on her composure and in order to hide her blushes, she stooped and administered a series of corrective pats and caresses to the unruly dogs.

'A very good gentleman of discernment you are,' old Bess cried delightedly as Jane gave her a look of embarrassed confusion. 'Are we then to know your name, sir?'

'I am John Fornton, the second son of my father, the Earl of Leyland.'

'I give you greetings, sir,' Jane said, extending her shapely white hand which he kissed with a little more warmth that was justifiable under the circumstances.

'I have heard of your father, a worthy gentleman and honoured by the late King, I believe.'

'Indeed, Lady Jane. He's the first of his name and family to hold the earldom, bestowed upon him by King Henry the Eighth.'

'And if I'm a judge of looks, the worthy father has a worthy son,' Bess put in giving John a look of frank appraisal.

John laughed and, bowing low, he replied, 'I try, good nurse, to be worthy of him.'

Bess seemed very pleased with herself and muttered in low tones, 'A most excellent, young gentleman, I swear. A man can't have such honest eyes and lack worthiness.'

It was John's turn now to feel a little confused as he heard the old nurse singing his praises. The fresh, whole-some colour of his face deepened somewhat, but Jane was not indifferent to his embarrassment and cleverly turned the conversation.

'Will you stay long with us, sir?' she asked.

'Unfortunately, no,' he said with a sigh. 'It is only by chance that we have the privilege of being here. My friend, William Alleyne, and I are travelling back to London, breaking our long journey at a coaching inn about two miles from here. Fortune directed one of your father's servants there and he asked us to the feast. Being strangers to

Sir George Holdenate, it would be a breach of the laws of hospitality to extend our visit beyond this morning. I'm now waiting for my friend's appearance, then we must leave.'

'Brief as your visit is, I would like you to take away a good impression of my home, sir. I was born here and have always lived here, so it's not unpardonable for me to feel very proud of it, is it? If it would not bore you, I should be pleased to show you the gardens. I say they are unsurpassed, but then I've seen very little of the world.'

An expression of ineffable delight came into John's face as he replied with his hand upon his heart, 'Lady Jane, I would be delighted.'

'Go on, you two, walk a while,' Bess stated with a big smile on her wrinkled face. 'My old limbs haven't the suppleness of yours.'

She sat down heavily on a convenient seat under an oak tree, while Jane and John moved away slowly accompanied by the frolicking dogs. It was a day when everything seemed to be golden and John listened with interest as Jane pointed out attractive features of the wonderful view. Her eyes were bright and clear and a faint smile tilted the edges of her mouth as she spoke enthusiastically.

John walked silently beside her, enthralled by the sun-touched sheen that gleamed on the dark tresses flowing out from below the caul, framing her perfect oval face. She was very lovely and at the same time there was an unsophisticated and unspoiled innocence about her that he had never found in any other woman. The hem of her gown brushed the short grass, making a hypnotic sound as they strolled and she spoke in a soft voice that was not only musical but held a sweetness that seemed almost to mesmerise him. The nearness of her made his heart beat painfully yet made a fool of his senses. He could no longer think clearly. He only knew that Lady Jane Holdenate was everything that was his ideal.

Suddenly aware that her visitor was strangely silent, she stopped and turned abruptly to find him gazing at her as if entranced. For a moment her eyes locked accusingly with his as she let out an outraged gasp.

'I declare, Master Fornton, you are not a bit interested and all my poor eloquence has been wasted.'

A short, drawn sigh escaped from John's lips.

'Lady, you do me wrong. I have indeed been deeply, deeply interested.'

'In the view? I think not, sir. It is shameful that you should wrong me. You presume upon your privilege as my father's guest.'

The words seemed to burst from her lips as she held up her hand to silence John's protest. He took her hand lightly and immediately felt her fingers tremble as he held them, but forced himself not to kiss the softness of her skin as he longed to do. He looked at her with hurt eyes and as the magnetism of his eyes drew hers, she looked up at him and their eyes held.

The two dogs, aware that their mistress had stopped, came charging back and leaped at Jane, causing her to lurch sideways. John instinctively stepped forward and threw his arm round her to hold her steady. There was a perceptible pause before either of them moved, then, obeying an impulse stronger than his will, his arms tightened around her and he felt her quiver with an unmistakable excitement that matched his own.

She was in his arms and he could resist her no longer as he lowered his head to find her lips. She remained motionless yet he knew as their lips touched that it was exactly right and he kissed her possessively yet reverently until he forgot everything but the magic of her lips and the softness and fragrance of her closeness. Only when he raised his head did John come to his sanity.

He was horrified at what he had done

but for the moment he was not certain what he should do about it. With a superhuman effort, he let his arms drop to his side and took a step backwards. What had possessed him to act so boldly? Lady Jane was spoken for! She was to be married to one of the most repulsive men he had ever known, yet that was no excuse. He had acted against the code of honour of a gentleman.

'Lady Jane, I am so ashamed of my lack of control. You must forget what happened just now. It was something that should never have occurred and I am so sorry,' he said hastily.

'Are you sorry you kissed me?' Jane asked in a soft voice.

'It was something that should never have happened.'

'But it did happen and interestingly you find it regrettable.'

John shook his head and looked away from her questioning eyes.

'It was foolish, and I deplore my error,' he stated unconvincingly. 'I can only beg for your forgiveness and that of your intended lord.'

As he spoke, he saw the colour leave her face and a look of unmistakable terror came into her eyes. He instinctively felt her alarm. He had put her in an uncompromising position. She was to be the wife of Sir Edward Sutton. He had no right to be here in the garden alone with her, no right at all. If only he were in Sir Edward's place! She must never know that kissing her had been the most wonderful thing he had experienced. It would serve no purpose. He must walk out of her life as quickly as he had walked in.

'It would be an impertinence for me to remain,' he stammered. 'I will not annoy you further by remaining here. Good day, Lady Jane.'

He paused as they approached Bess, but the dear old soul was dozing peacefully under the tree. He knew that it was useless to prolong the meeting yet what could he do to smooth the situation? Jane made no attempt to respond and slowly turned her back to him. He turned back towards the house. As he reached the upper garden, he was relieved to find William had risen and was speaking to Sir George. Greetings were exchanged and John thanked his host for allowing them to enjoy the famous hospitality of Ladsill.

'We are extremely privileged to have enjoyed your regal hospitality, Sir George,' John began. 'Speaking for myself, I feel very fortunate that I have made the acquaintance of your daughter, Lady Jane.'

'My daughter?' Sir George asked in surprised agitation.

'Yes, sir, I have had the honour of her company in the garden just now.'

Sir George's face suddenly became unreadable, only his smile remained ruthlessly in place.

'I will delay you no longer, sirs. Trusting that your plans and future journeying will be beneficial, I bid you good-day.'

With this dismissive statement, Sir

George turned and walked away.

'I would say that Sir George is not in agreement to you showing favour to his daughter, my friend,' William stated with a grin as they mounted their steeds and rode off. 'The sooner we leave here the better, if you ask me.'

3

Jane stood silently staring over the view trying to calm her palpitating heart. Why had he kissed her then said it was a mistake, an error? Was that all it was to him — a blunder, a momentary slip? Her lips still tingled from the shock of his kiss yet to him it was an indiscretion that he would no doubt soon forget about. She gave an uncontrolled sob. She could have enjoyed his chivalrous company.

It wasn't every day she had the chance to talk to a handsome young cavalier. Why couldn't Sir Edward be more like him, then she would not object to their betrothal? In fact the idea of being betrothed to Master Fornton had great appeal. She nursed this idea to herself but knew it to be an impossible dream. He had told her to forget the incident and she must.

With a regretful sigh, she turned away but the sound of idle laughter and snippets of colourful chatter floating on the wind prompted her to turn back and stretch forward to look over the balustrade. By the path that led to the garden gate, two or three gardeners and female servants were grouped together evidently very interested in a singular-looking woman, to whom they were listening with great interest. One of the gardeners caught sight of Jane and drew away from the group, respectfully greeting the mistress of the house. The others followed suit but Jane's attention was arrested by the appearance of the strange woman in their group.

She was tall and picturesquely garbed in a gown made up of various coloured clothes. Her skin was almost bronze, proclaiming her Eastern origin, and on her head she wore a faded red kerchief from which escaped untidy strands of jet black hair. A large plain gold ring was suspended from the unusually large lobes of each of her ears and she wore numerous bangles round her arms and ankles which, like her feet, were bare.

'Stay where you are, woman. I will not harm you,' Jane ordered in a voice of authority. 'Just tell me your business here or I will have you arrested as a gipsy robber.'

The woman eyed her suspiciously yet there was no fright in her defiant stance or those black eyes that flashed like shards of polished marble. For a long minute Jane and the stranger stared at each other as if they were both under the influence of some irresistible fascination.

'She is a fortune teller, Lady Jane, if it so please you,' one of the gardeners said.

'A fortune teller,' the stranger repeated with a contemptuous toss of her head. 'I read the stars and see things that few mortals see. I can predict death and reveal the future. I can cast spells, and bring a person to me though he is hundreds of miles away. I have strange powers that make me able to foretell the future.'

The servants were impressed, although a sense of fear made them keep their distance; but Lady Jane Holdenate was an educated, highly-cultured, intelligent young lady and therefore she didn't regard this strange creature with the same superstitious awe. The woman might be an impostor, but she was certainly a very interesting one.

Jane returned to the sleeping Bess, who moaned as she raised herself and looked around as if in a daze.

'Have I missed anything?' she asked in surprise. 'Where is Master Fornton?'

'He had to leave,' Jane said in defiant tones.

'Leave so soon?' the old nurse questioned studying Jane's flushed face. 'I would have like to talk to him. Let us hope your father invites him back soon. He seems a very agreeable young man, very agreeable indeed. Now, if your father had chosen Master Fornton for your betrothed I . . . '

'Stop it, Bess. Stop it.'

Jane's voice whipped out in anger and frustration leaving old Bess rather concerned and confused. Had something happened between them? If he had laid a finger on her — no, he was a gentleman. If Bess hadn't been so sure of that fact she would never have allowed them to walk together unchaperoned. She had an unerring instinct about such things, a kind of intuitive faculty of appraising the virtues and vices of the opposite sex. Something in John Fornton's eyes, his looks, his voice and manners made old Bess pronounce him satisfactory, unlike Sir Edward.

'We have another visitor in the lower garden,' Jane said, anxious to change the conversation.

'In the lower garden? What sort of visitor comes into the lower garden? You'll be telling me next, they came in through the garden gate.'

'Being uninvited, yes, she probably did,' Jane said with a grin. 'She's a fortune teller. Should we summon her here and see what she can predict?'

Bess shook her head.

'Nay, my pet. I don't like the sound of her. A fortune teller? You shouldn't encourage such people. Surely you can't believe in that kind of thing.'

'Is anyone ever really free from superstition or belief in supernatural powers?' Jane laughed. 'Do say we can invite her to tell our fortunes. It would amuse me, Bess.'

'What use have we for a fortune teller? I am too old and as for you, my pet, your future was settled yesterday with your betrothal to Sir Edward.'

Jane's head drooped and she hunched her shoulders in a defeated manner which pulled at the heartstrings of old Bess who relented enough to walk down the garden to take a closer look at the strange creature who could tell fortunes.

'Upon my word,' Bess whispered eyeing the woman with interest.

Jane gave Bess a confident smile and, against Bess's better judgement, requested the visitor to join them in the main garden. Settling themselves on a bench in the shade of the honeysuckle bower they watched as the stranger advanced towards them, her skirts swishing, her bangles flashing and a huge crystal, suspended from an adder skin round her neck, glowing with violet and red fire. A short distance from the two ladies, she stopped.

'Come closer, woman,' Bess ordered and the woman obediently took a couple more steps forward.

Her eyes washed slowly over Bess then came to rest on Jane. She stared at her with eyes that seemed to peer into her very soul. One minute they were dull, vacant, and so dreamy they seemed almost lifeless, the next they shone with a fierce, gleaming light. This strange woman was no commonplace person. She was evidently a person of keen, alert intelligence and in an age when credulity, ignorance and superstition were universal, it was not difficult for such a woman to pose as one possessed of supernatural gifts.

'What is your name?' Jane asked speaking directly to the woman.

'Jedaan. Some call me Jedaan, the prophetess. Jedaan of the tribe of Ali, magicians and seers.'

'A pretty name,' Jane added in a hospitable manner. 'I would like to know more about you, Jedaan, and put your boasted powers to the test.'

'I can tell you much. I see strange things in your eyes and your hand is like a book. All that has been and will be is written there,' Jedaan said in a hollow tone.

She looked at Jane keenly for several silent moments then she spoke in a slow and pleasant voice.

'You have a great beauty, lady, beauty of no common order, and you are sweet-minded and gentle like the doves cooing in yonder trees.'

Jane's face reddened as Jedaan moved forward and stretched out a dark-skinned hand towards her.

'Give me your hand, fair lady. I like you. You have a good face and an honest eye, an eye to burn men's hearts and subdue their souls.'

Jane extended her small white hand which the woman grasped between her own brown ones, then pressed it to her lips. She turned it over and manipulated it for a few moments as if gauging its size, the length of the fingers and the quality of the skin.

'Ah!' she muttered mysteriously, as she studied the palm.

The way she uttered the interjection conveyed a world of meaning, and aroused in Jane and Bess a keen curiosity and a desire to know what lay behind it.

'What do you see in my hand?' Jane asked with a nervous smile.

'It's a pretty hand,' Jedaan said thoughtfully, 'and a hand worthy of so sweet a body. You are a great lady yet a strange future lies before you.'

'Have a care, woman,' Bess said lightly. 'Don't insult our intelligence.'

Jedaan continued unconcerned.

'You will marry.'

'A very safe prophecy,' Bess remarked. 'I think I could have prophesied so much.'

'He whose bride you will be will be none of your father's choosing,' Jedaan continued, indifferent to the taunts. 'Aye, he will come in secret and his coming will change the fortunes of this house. He will take control when the present lord can rule no more.'

'Peace, Jedaan,' Jane cried, pulling her hand away hastily as she saw her father and Sir Edward advancing towards them.

Jedaan stood like a statue, apparently impassive and unmoved by the two men who stared at her in disbelief.

'Before God,' Sir George cried looking baffled, 'whom have we here? A wandering lunatic surely.'

Sir Edward chuckled with sycophantic laughter and Jedaan instantly fixed him with her piercing eyes. With an easy style she took one pace towards him and Sir Edward stopped laughing instantly as his expression changed to one of alarm.

'This is Jedaan, my lord father,' Jane replied. 'She is a prophetess.'

'A prophetess? An impostor and a cheat, I'll warrant, and one who will come to the ducking stool or have to stand the witch's ordeal.'

A gleam of fire shone from Jedaan's black eyes, and her stained teeth were revealed as her full, moist red lips parted in a smile of contempt.

'I am no witch nor am I an impostor or cheat. I have powers that have come to me through a long line of ancestors all similarly gifted, powers to foretell the future. I see things that are to be. I don't weave destinies.'

'Which is very forbearing of you,' Sir George remarked sarcastically. 'Here, witch, tell me what you see in my hand.'

As he spoke, he tossed Jedaan a silver groat from his purse.

'Nay, sir. I will not take your money but I will give this gentleman some information.'

She stared at Sir Edward with her intent gaze, then peered into the crystal that hung from the adder skin round her neck. She spoke in a hollow, faraway voice.

'You are not married.'

'Not yet but . . . '

'Nor will you ever be.'

'Rubbish. The Lady Jane and I are betrothed. Only yesterday we celebrated.'

'It was not this fair lady who shared your bed last night.'

Sir George exhaled in a noisy fashion before turning to Jane.

'Why did you bring such a stupid creature to the garden, Jane? Get off my land, wretch, or I'll set the dogs on you.'

'No, Father,' Jane pleaded.

She had been noticeably stunned by the disclosure but she would not allow her father to hound Jedaan for daring to make such a bold allegation.

'We can't send this woman away empty. It would augur ill for us and

71

would not be in accordance with Ladsill's hospitality.'

'Then for once the laws of Ladsill's hospitality will be broken,' Sir George replied regaining his composure. 'Go hence, woman. I don't like your looks.'

With a single dismissive jerk of his arm, Sir George summoned the captain of the guard who appeared almost at once.

'See that this woman leaves my property immediately,' he ordered. 'I don't want a prig here.'

'I am no prig,' Jedaan retorted, glaring at Sir George then she spun round to the guard who had taken a bold step towards her. 'Don't you dare touch me or I'll paralyse you where you stand,' she spat at him as she fixed him with her eyes.

The man looked unsure and at a loss what to do. He was a powerful man but he was no match for Jedaan. She gracefully crossed her arms over her bosom, bowed her head twice to Jane and glared at Sir Edward who had remained a silent spectator of the scene. Then with stately, slow steps she walked away. The assembled group remained silent, watching Jedaan and the escort until they were out of sight.

'The woman was mad,' Sir Edward declared with a shaky laugh.

'Was she, my lord?' Jane asked giving him a look that would freeze water. 'I guess we will never know. Strange though, I thought she was very eloquent. I had no difficulty in understanding my prophecy. Did you think she was insane, Bess?'

'No, my lady,' the old nurse stammered trying to unwind the happenings of the last few minutes in her own mind.

'No more of this senseless chatter. Come, Jane, Sir Edward and I fancy a spot of hawking. Will you join us?'

Sir George draped his arm round his daughter's shoulders. Jane's first reaction was to feign a headache or other pressing engagement then she changed her mind. A good fast gallop with the feel of the wind in her hair always proved enjoyable, and she wouldn't allow the fact that Sir Edward was there to detract from her pleasure. She simply would not allow it.

'Yes, father,' she replied defiantly with a toss of her head, 'my merlins must be given exercise. I will change and join you presently. Will you arrange for my palfrey to be saddled ready? Come, Bess.'

The old nurse rose obediently from the seat and, stiff with rheumatism, hobbled after her ward. Jane checked her pace, walking thoughtfully by Bess's side back to the Hall.

'What do you make of that, Bess? Do you think Jedaan invents stories for our amusement or could there be some truth in her words?'

'I'm sure I don't know, my pet. I'd like to think that she was right about you not marrying Sir Edward, who was your father's choice, particularly after what she said about where he was last night. I'm surprised your father didn't call him out.'

'No, my father could hardly act on the word of a gipsy woman even if he wanted to. Men like female company, particularly men like Sir Edward. It wouldn't surprise me if he leaves a string of bastards in his wake.'

'Lady Jane,' Bess gasped in horror. 'That is not the kind of thing a lady should know of let alone speak about. Your poor, dear mother would turn in her grave. How do you know of such things?'

'I listen to the maids and village girls. Apparently the daughter of the landlord of The Peacock, Mary I think they call her, is only too willing to . . .'

'Jane, stop it! I will not allow you to say such things. You are prattling like a scullery maid. Remember who you are!'

'How could I forget? I am cosseted away and kept in ignorance. It is all right for me to be betrothed but I am completely ignorant of any matters to do with men. It seems that it's all right for men to get experience first hand but

I can't even ask questions. A scullery maid would know what to expect and what was expected of her on her wedding night but not me.'

'There, there, my pet. Have no fear. You'll know what to do naturally when the time comes.'

'I doubt it, Bess. Even the thought of holding hands with Sir Edward is repulsive to me so how can I let him touch me?'

Bess sniffed.

'You'll change your mind as you get to know him better.'

'I don't want to get to know him better. I can't stand the sight of him.'

'Then why are you going hawking with him?'

'I'm going with my father. Just because Sir Edward is in the party doesn't mean that I have to give up one of my pleasures. I intend to ignore him the entire time.'

'Would you ignore Master Fornton if he was in the party?'

Bess smiled testily as she watched

with interest the reaction her words provoked. Jane flashed her a confused look as the colour heightened in her cheeks.

'It would be very rude of me to ignore a guest who is unfamiliar with the local terrain.'

'Is that the only reason?'

'Of course. Stop this prattling and help me out of these clothes. By the time I'm ready it will be too late to go at this rate.'

The head falconer and other servants were busy with the preparations as the small group assembled in the courtyard ready for the afternoon's sport. Jane stroked the soft, downy nose of her little pony, Belitha, and spoke to her gently before being helped into her side saddle. A maid arranged Jane's flowing skirts in preparation for the ride and as Sir Edward and Sir George mounted, their example was followed by the servants going along.

Slowly the riders set off across the courtyard, through the main gates and out on to the pitted track. In single file they crossed the stone bridge spanning the whispering river, then the pace quickened as the track widened. Sir George rode at her side and on his gauntletted wrist sat his prize peregrine falcon. She was a haggard, a wild hawk caught in full adult plumage, which he had captured and laboriously trained himself. On Jane's wrist, balancing with a firm grip of talons and secured by jesses, sat one of the head falconer's home-bred birds that would also be put through its paces. Branching off from the main highway the riders galloped through the lush meadowland then plunged into the woods that fringed the grassland, imprisoning the riders between tall trees and thickets.

Some leaves had begun to fall and soon others would follow, forming a thick carpet on the forest floor. The horse's hooves thundered along in easy rhythm and shouts of pleasure echoed through the woods. Then moorland extended as far as the eye could see, punctured only intermittently by shrubs and trees and a few dry grey rocks that stabbed through the course earth. This was hawking country.

A thinly-clouded sky, opalescent with hidden sunshine, heralded the approach of autumn, giving even the flat moors a wild beauty that Jane found exciting. Belitha was tiny but fleet of foot. Jane had developed into a fine horsewoman and the promise of an afternoon's sport could not be dulled by the presence of Sir Edward.

On Jane's wrist, her unfledged hawk sat motionless within her hood, from where she could fix her stare on everything that moved, ready and waiting for that moment when the hood would be slipped off and she would be free. An anticipatory thrill passed through the assembled group as the dogs flushed out the prey. Instantly the waiting hawks were released and all eyes were strained upwards. Jane urged Belitha forward, her long hair streaming behind her like a silken banner.

In the air, the birds rose higher and higher until they were mere specks, then, like thunderbolts, the hawks were dropping on their prey. The remainder of the field ran or rode to be in at the kill, but Jane reigned in and sat in agitated silence waiting and watching until the sound of their voices faded in the distance and the echo of hoofbeats was swallowed up by the coarse undergrowth. She found the thrill of the chase exhilarating although once the hawks had performed their triumphant ritual, she preferred to hold back from the carnage. Shielding her eyes in an attempt to see into the distance, she failed to notice the lone rider advancing towards her.

'Greetings, Lady Jane.'

The friendly, male voice made her start and she whirled round to see John Fornton reigning in his horse beside her. As he spoke, he removed his plumed hat and gave a deep bow. Jane fought hard to hide the pleasure this unexpected meeting gave her.

'Greetings, Master Fornton,' she said, shakily offering him her hand.

As soon as he took it and raised it slowly to his lips, his touch precipitated a peculiar reaction that she found hard to explain.

'This is indeed an unexpected pleasure that we should meet again, Lady Jane,' he drawled softly, his eyes scrutinising the perfect oval face framed with unruly locks that cascaded freely down her back.

To John's enraptured gaze she looked more like an angel than a human person. Jane lowered her head, bashfully aware of what had transpired during their last meeting. She peeped through half-closed lashes as the tiny buttons down the front of his doublet flashed in the bright sunlight, noting how he moved self-consciously to straighten the silk brocade cloak thrown casually over one broad shoulder.

'May I escort you to your father?' he asked politely but Jane gave an emphatic shake of her pretty head.

'There really is no need, Master Fornton,' she replied abruptly. 'I prefer to watch from a distance, thank you.'

John could not hide his delight but keeping his voice steady he spoke.

'Then may I offer you my company until your party returns?'

Giving him a coy glance she nodded her agreement.

'You would be most welcome to join us if you partake of this sport, sir.'

'Thank you, Lady Jane,' he replied with obvious disappointment. 'Perhaps another time. I'm on my way to Migfield Manor where I'll be meeting my travelling companion, William Alleyne, and from there we travel to London.'

'Why Migfield Manor, my lord? Surely that is the home of Lord and Lady Turbot.'

'Indeed it is. Lady Turbot is my sister.'

'Your sister? Lady Turbot was a good friend of my mother's. I've spent much time at Migfield Manor with Lady Turbot and your young nieces and nephews. How many do you have now, four?'

'Five with the new baby, an addition I'll be seeing in due course.'

'How wonderful. I envy those with large families. I'm an only child and I always wanted brothers and sisters so I'm determined to have a large family. I'll have at least two boys and two . . . '

Jane paused in horror. She couldn't believe that she had brought up such a delicate subject and spoken in such a manner to a complete stranger. She felt her blush rising until it coloured her entire face in confusion.

'I beg your pardon, my lord. I really shouldn't . . . I don't know why . . . '

'Please, don't be sorry. You have said nothing to be sorry for. I have four brothers and a sister so for me I can't begin to imagine what it must be like to be an only child.'

Jane rewarded him with a silent smile as the thunder of galloping hooves announced the arrival of Sir Edward Sutton. He was riding so fast that as he halted, the horse was nearly thrown on his haunches. Jane noticed the disapproving look John flung at Sir Edward and the equally hostile look thrown by Sir Edward. Neither man made any attempt to openly acknowledge the other and Jane looked from one to the other in surprise.

Sir Edward thrust Jane's falcon at her as if it were an inanimate object. The bird settled almost immediately on her arm. Jane smoothed the falcon's ruffled plumage and secured its jesses without comment. A tiny smirk lightened the habitual severity of Sir Edward's expression.

'Come, my lady,' he ordered, circling round to the head of her palfrey. 'Your father and the rest of the field are waiting for you.'

In the manner that one would guide a child on its first pony, Sir Edward took hold of Belitha's reign, dug his heavy metal spurs into his horse's dapple grey flanks and set off back up the moor. Jane and John exchanged swift glances as she had no alternative but to ride off with Sir Edward.

'Who is that strutting gallant? You seem to know him, Lady Jane. What is his name?' Sir Edward asked as they neared the rest of the group.

'If you hadn't dragged me away so rudely, I would have introduced you.'

Jane's voice rose on an angry note.

'I had no wish to meet him, just to know his name and question why he should detain you in conversation when you are with a hawking party.'

'You know only too well that it was my choice to stay back and watch from a distance. I didn't expect him to keep me company. It was by sheer coincidence that he happened to be passing on his way to Migfield Manor.'

'Who is on his way to Migfield Manor?' Sir George asked walking his horse over to join them as they reigned in.

'Master John Fornton,' Jane faltered.

'He was at the celebrations yesterday evening.'

'Of course. I remember Master Fornton, son of the Earl of Leyland. His sister is Lady Turbot of Migfield Manor. I believe you and he met in the garden this morning, my daughter.'

Jane nodded, then dropped her eyes but not before she had seen the disagreeable look on Sir Edward's harsh face.

'The garden seemed pretty busy with uninvited guests this morning, Sir George. Do you allow every wandering nobody to simply stroll into your garden and converse with your daughter? A witch, an itinerant — how many more intruders have you entertained there, Lady Jane?'

'Master Fornton was our guest, Sir Edward.' The icy note in Sir George's tone was now evident as he stared at Sir Edward. 'Whom I wish to entertain and invite to my home is my concern and mine alone. I would ask that you remember that in future. When you become the Lord of Ladsill Hall you will do as you please. In the meantime, I would advise you to curb your tongue. If Master Fornton is still in the vicinity, I'm sure you will feel duty bound to apologise for what I can only assume was a rather hostile encounter.'

'No, sir. If that is John Fornton, son of the Earl of Leyland, time for apology has passed. I have a score to settle with that young man.'

4

'You seem rather out of sorts, my friend. Are you sickening for something or still thinking about the lovely Lady Jane?' William Alleyne asked, giving his friend a sidelong look as they rode away from Migfield Manor.

With mock levity, John pressed his hand on his heart.

'I fear both, Will,' he replied, wearing a soulful expression. 'I think my heart will remain for ever at Ladsill Hall, but how can I declare my love for a lady whose heart is pledged elsewhere?'

'John, my dear fellow, if I didn't know you better I would question this line of talk. From your tone I could almost believe you to be serious, but I know you of old. At the very next inn, you'll find a pleasant serving wench who will only need to smile and your heart will be hers.'

'If only I could agree with you, my friend,' John smirked before falling back into his melancholy. 'I was just wondering for the hundredth time why Lady Jane is betrothed to Sir Edward Sutton. They are not at all suited. He is impetuous and hasty and has made numerous enemies, while she is sweet and shy and . . . '

'Say no more, my friend. It has not gone unnoticed that you are besotted with the lady but what do you know of Sir Edward?' William added thoughtfully.

John's face took on a hard expression as he stared ahead.

'He's a bigoted thinker whose name has been linked with a plot against the Princess Elizabeth. On discovery of the plot, Sir Edward Sutton denounced all his associates and had several, who may have proved dangerous to him, secretly assassinated.'

'He sounds a very unscrupulous man,' William added showing no great surprise.

'He's as unscrupulous as he is unprincipled,' John snorted in rage, 'and then you wonder why I am concerned about his betrothal to that sweet creature.'

They rode along in silence until they reached the village of Rowton where a picturesque inn with a broad bowling-green tempted them to halt. Hardly an hour later, the distant sound of galloping horses drew their attention and in the direction from which they had come, a cloud of dust heralded the approach of three horsemen who checked their pace suddenly at the front of the inn. A large, unwieldy, red-faced man flung himself from his horse, followed by his companions, a young coxcomb and a rather gloomy-looking, middle-aged esquire.

'Landlord,' the red-faced gentleman roared in blustering tones, 'send your ostler to our steeds. I have a score to settle with one of your customers.'

The landlord scurried out from the interior of the inn, looking a little scared at the prospect of a quarrel.

'I would humbly crave to know your name and quality, sir,' the landlord said, looking at the mismatched trio and particularly at the rather large gentleman who glared back unpleasantly.

'I am Sir Edward Sutton, this is my friend Sir Ralph Bandale and my esquire,' he replied, throwing his reigns to an ostler.

'And whom do you seek, sir? the landlord asked.

'John Fornton, who with false tongue has slandered my name. He will answer to me with his life.'

John Fornton, who had overheard this, came forward and, recognising Sir Edward, bowed low.

'John Fornton, at your service, Sir Edward.'

'You, John Fornton, I charge with being a false and perjured slanderer,' Sir Edward stated.

'On what authority?' John asked proudly.

'On the authority of Hubert Armstrong, landlord. Has he spoken the truth or lied when he says you have defamed me?'

'If Armstrong reported me as saying that you have a reputation for being clever in deceit, then he has reported truly.'

'Then by the Mother of God,' Sir Edward cried in a towering rage, 'you shall make good your words with your sword, unless you are a white-livered poltroon, afraid in case your fair skin should be scratched. In that case, I'll split you like a woodcock. I give you challenge.'

As he said this, he flung his riding gloves with great force in John's face. John hardly winced then, kicking the glove away, drew his sword.

'You will have your revenge, Sir Knight,' John sneered. 'On your guard, Sir Edward, for today, by God's mercy, Lady Jane Holdenate shall be freed from the possibility of becoming your wife. You are not even fit to fasten the latchet on her shoe.'

This taunt maddened Sir Edward.

'The devil receive you,' he shouted as he made a desperate lunge at his antagonist, who skilfully parried the thrust.

With a brave leap, William Alleyne was between the combatants and struck their swords aside.

'What do you mean by this outrage?' he cried to Sir Edward.

'Stand to one side, dolt,' Sir Edward roared, 'or I'll strike my sword through your body.'

'Dolt!' William cried angrily. 'I am no dolt! I'm a gentleman of quality and honour. My friend's quarrel is mine also.'

'Your name and rank, sir?' the young Sir Ralph Bandale demanded as he rushed to his friend's aid.

'My name is William Alleyne, esquire and gentleman of fortune. And yours?'

'Sir Ralph Bandale, son of Sir Hope Bandale, a gentleman of fortune and a man of honour.'

'No, Will,' John cried in a passionate appeal. 'This quarrel is mine alone. It's between the two of us, so stay out of it.'

Before William could reply, Sir Ralph flung his glove into William's face.

'My friend's quarrel is mine also, therefore, on guard,' he challenged.

'On guard,' Sir Edward shouted as he aimed another blow at John.

The four men now fought in deadly earnest and quite a crowd gathered to watch the action because it was not often that the sleepy village was disturbed by the clash of steel and the cries of half-maddened combatants. For some minutes the swordsmen fought with determination and skill while thrust and parry struck sparks of fire from the well-tempered steel.

The onlookers quickly selected their favourites and the balance of opinion inclined to the side of John Fornton and his friend. The odds on John, however, were very small, for although he appeared to be the better swords-man, Sir Edward had ponderous strength and great weight behind him and it was thought that this would tell in striking down his antagonist's guard, and getting home a disabling or fatal thrust.

In the case of William Alleyne and Sir Ralph Bandale, there were hardly two opinions. Sir Ralph was a slight, delicate youth who displayed no great skill, whereas William was an expert swordsman and it was noted that he was restraining himself with a view to exhausting his opponent and then disarming him. Unflattering chance remarks from the crowd were overheard by an infuriated Sir Ralph who made a sudden furious onslaught on his opponent. William nearly lost his footing and could do nothing but guard himself. At last, however, he recovered his position and by a very skilful blow he slightly wounded his foe in the shoulder.

'First blood,' William cried, 'and since you and I have no cause for quarrel, let us put up our swords, Sir Ralph.'

The young dandy briefly examined his shoulder, snorting out a defiant epithet then continued to rain blows at William who eventually decided that the only way to stop this young fire-eater was to disarm him by wounding him in the sword arm. But Sir Ralph made a sudden lunge and rush. The lunge was parried, William thrust, Sir Ralph failed to guard himself and the point of William's sword went deep into his chest. He fell back with a gurgling cry and was instantly picked up and laid on a bench were attempts were made to staunch the blood.

The struggle for mastery between the other two men grew more furious and desperate. The perspiration ran down their faces, their clothes were disordered, their hair dishevelled. Their breath came thick and fast, their eyes gleaming with the fire of hate. This was a fight to the death and each knew it.

Nimbly side-stepping to avoid a well-aimed thrust, John slipped on a stone and momentarily lost his balance, giving Sir Edward his opportunity. With a rapid thrust, he ran his sword through his opponent's shoulder and John's weapon fell to the ground. He would have followed if his servant hadn't rushed forward and caught him.

Although Sir Edward was flushed and elated by his victory, he became furious when he learned that his friend was dead. He had travelled with him from the lad's home in Cheshire, brought him as a guest to Ladsill and now this fatal termination placed Sir Edward in a most unhappy position. He cursed his impetuosity and bitterly blamed himself for not having prevented the hot-headed youth from rushing to his doom. Sir Edward had a litter hastily constructed and the body was borne away in a melancholy procession.

John Fornton, grievously wounded, was carried to an upper chamber of the hostelry while the small crowd that had gathered seemed in no hurry to leave the scene. It soon became generally known that Sir Edward had followed John Fornton and challenged him to combat. Mutterings of anger against Sir Edward Sutton spread quickly round the sleepy hamlet but these simple-living villagers were well aware that it was not wise for them to interfere in the quarrels of persons of quality, so they discussed the excitement of the day amongst themselves.

The sturdy blacksmith was of the opinion that Sir Edward had fought foul and expressed this opinion to the little cobbler who bemoaned the fact that he had not witnessed the event. He in turn related the happenings to a peddler passing through who spread the news as he went. Soon it was known for miles around that the sleepy hamlet had been the scene of a fight between some cavaliers and that the son of the Earl of Leyland was lying at the inn in Rowton, wounded to death.

Jedaan heard of the fight and its results with interest and as the sun departed in an ocean of flaming colour and the moon rose, she made her way through the valley. The village slept as

Jedaan made her way silently towards the inn where the thin light from a couple of meadow rushes flickered from the latticed window of John Fornton's room.

Suddenly, the peace was shattered as William, sitting watching his wounded friend, heard a woman's voice clamouring for admittance to the inn. The landlord, irritated at being disturbed from his rest, armed himself with a ponderous blunderbuss, and from an open window demanded to know who it was who disturbed the peace of the night.

'Give me admission,' Jedaan demanded impressively. 'I need to see the wounded gentleman.'

'Wait while I don my clothes,' the landlord replied knowing that the wounded gentleman was a man of quality with a well-lined purse.

He had no fear that he would be well repaid for any trouble or inconvenience he was caused. Unbarring the heavy door to admit Jedaan, he was a little alarmed to see this strange visitor.

'Do you know the hurt gentleman?' he asked in some trepidation.

'Aye,' she answered with curt brusqueness.

'Have you skills in medicines and the dressing of wounds?'

'Aye,' she answered again.

'Has the gentleman knowledge of your coming?'

'Cease this babble and conduct me to him,' she commanded and the landlord was so awed that his hand began to tremble as he held his fluttering lantern aloft and guided her up the narrow stairs to the top room where John lay.

Both William and John were amazed and rather annoyed to see the strange creature suddenly thrust into their company.

'What is your business and why are you here at such an hour, woman?' William demanded.

'My name is Jedaan and I'm here to give comfort,' she announced never taking her eyes from John.

100

'I need it,' John replied with a feeble sigh. 'I feel my life is ebbing.'

'Nay, sir, your time of departure is not yet,' Jedaan replied solemnly. 'Let me see the wound.'

As Jedaan stepped forward, William stood up to bar her way, protesting that a woman from the village had already dressed it and as soon as the day broke, a servant was to ride to the nearby town and bring back a surgeon. From the bed John let out a low groan.

'My own skills are not inferior to those of a surgeon and maybe superior,' Jedaan assured him. 'I'm also sure that I can give him ease and restful sleep, which will lessen the chance of a fever.'

William was unconvinced but without a sound, John slowly pushed away the coverlet. With extraordinary dexterity and delicacy of touch, Jedaan removed his bandages and examined the wound with a critical eye.

''Tis a clean wound, though a painful one,' she stated producing a small bag of untanned leather from under her petticoat.

The contents of the bag were a miscellaneous selection. There were phials filled with coloured liquids, some white flax, a metal box containing a green ointment, and what seemed to be pieces of bark of the alder or willow tree. She bathed the wound with water from an ewer that stood nearby then on to the wound she poured a few drops of lotion from one of her phials. This evidently produced some smarting as the patient winced in pain.

Next, she soaked a pad of flax with some lotion and drawing the edges of the wound together, she cleverly bound the flax on it with a piece of the bark straightened out. The dressing complete, she gave John a drink from one of the other phials, then sat back to watch the effect of her treatment. John became drowsy and within an hour was fast asleep. Jedaan relaxed, then, telling William to rest, she curled up in the corner of the room, wrapped her scarf round her head and slumbered soundly.

There were many versions of the story which flew round the neighbourhood like wild fire. The generally accepted one was that the combat had been between Sir Edward Sutton and Master John Fornton owing to the latter having attacked the reputation of the former. However, another version stated that the combat had been between rivals for the hand of one of the country's most beautiful women, Lady Jane Holdenate.

Sir George Holdenate heard the account of the fight first hand when, upon his return to Ladsill Hall, Sir Edward Sutton asked for a private interview with him. Sir Edward, needless to say, told his own version of the story, emphasising the fact that his own reputation had suffered by Fornton's slander, and honour demanded that he should be challenged. Sir George retained a diplomatic silence intending to make his own enquiries into the matter.

He was strongly opposed to such hasty appeal to arms when explanations might have set matters right. He took a far more serious view of matters than Sir Edward was disposed to do and expressed grave fears that the powerful Bandale family would not let the affair rest where it was. The body of Sir Ralph Bandale had been left at a neighbouring village overnight ready to be transported back to be laid in the family tomb with all the pomp and ceremony befitting one of his station.

After speaking to Sir George, Sir Edward Sutton sought out Jane and informed her that he would be leaving Ladsill Hall at first light. He gave no indication as to why he was leaving sooner than expected and Jane, surprised yet enormously relieved, didn't care to ask. If he was foolish enough to suppose that she would remain in ignorance of the event, he had not bargained for the news being discussed by the servants.

It had been brought to the Hall by a

butcher who supplied the family with small meats and his information was that there had been a fierce encounter between some gentlemen. One was killed and Master Fornton had been wounded by his opponent. When old Bess, with eager interest, enquired the cause of the quarrel, Syd Dawson, the head forester, declared that he'd wager a year's wage there was a woman at the bottom of it. The old nurse looked uneasy and motioned to Syd Dawson her wish to speak to him in private.

'Tell no-one,' she whispered to a surprised Syd Dawson, 'but ride hard to Rowton and bring me a report of Master John Fornton and mark you, Syd, let it be a true report, even if it tells of his death.'

'What is John Fornton to thee, Bess?' Syd Dawson asked with interest.

'It concerns thee not, Syd Dawson. Now go lest I seek another to do this service,' Bess snapped, giving him a stern look.

Syd questioned no further and within

half an hour was off on his errand. Meanwhile Bess made her way to Jane's chamber.

'Have you seen Sir Edward this evening?' she asked gently as she took the brush and began brushing Jane's long hair.

'Yes, briefly,' Jane replied. 'He seemed in a fearful hurry and announced he would be leaving at first light.'

'But did he say anything else to you?' Bess coaxed. 'Anything at all?'

'Oh, much, but of such little importance that I've forgotten it all. There was one thing I remember he said — I was to dream of him. Bess, if I were to dream of him, I would have nightmares,' she added with a shudder.

'Would you rather dream of handsome John Fornton, eh?' Bess asked, but Jane turned and walked towards the window, expressing a fear that the weather was going to change.

'Would you like news of Master Fornton?' the old nurse asked, watching

Jane with troubled concern.

'I don't particularly care, Bess, although I have a woman's curiosity if you know something of interest.'

'John Fornton is lying grievously wounded.'

'Grievously wounded?' Jane echoed, turning abruptly from the window.

'So runs the report,' Bess stated, now having Jane's undivided attention.

'Who has wounded him?'

'Sir Edward Sutton.'

'What!' Jane was shocked. 'He said nothing to me of this.'

'No, I didn't think he would.'

'Is that why he is leaving, because of this quarrel?'

'Not exactly,' the old nurse stated, choosing her words carefully. 'Sir Edward brought a friend, Sir Ralph Bandale, with him this visit.'

'Yes, a popinjay who swaggers and struts like my dear old peacock.'

'Well, Sir Ralph is dead.'

'Dead?' Jane exclaimed in horror. 'Who killed him? John Fornton?'

'No, not John Fornton but his friend, William Alleyne, so the gossip says. Supposedly Sir Edward Sutton set about John Fornton and when William Alleyne took his friend's part, Sir Ralph Bandale set about William Alleyne, who slayed him. Sir Edward is to carry the body back to Cheshire to the boy's home. That is why he must leave without a delay.'

'How terrible. But what was the cause of the quarrel, Bess?' Jane asked deeply disturbed.

'I don't know for sure. There are many reports. Some say a woman is involved,' Bess replied gently trying to spare her mistress too much distress while at the same time imparting all the relevant information. 'Jane, I think that woman could be you.'

'Me? Why?' she asked puzzled, thinking for a moment. 'Do you think that John Fornton spoke ill of me and Sir Edward . . . '

'Nay, my lady,' Bess interrupted emphatically. 'I think not. What man would speak ill of you?'

'Oh, Bess, you are silly. Not everyone sees with your eyes or thinks your thoughts,' Jane said trying to smile.

'No, my pet,' old Bess cried. 'If they did, Sir Edward Sutton would have found no welcome under this roof.'

Jane cast a reproving glance at her doting old nurse.

'Why did you say the quarrel could be because of me, Bess? I don't know John Fornton.'

'More's the pity,' the kindly old soul said, who would willingly have laid her life down for her charge. 'He would have made you a good partner which is more than can be said for Sir Edward. I saw the way he looked at you. My old eyes are not that dim nor my senses so blunted that I don't see fire in a young man's eyes when he sees a pretty girl. I see no fire in Sir Edward's eyes; they are cold and calculating and greedy. You're too gentle and sweet and beautiful for such as he. I couldn't stand it if you were forced into the arms of that bear.'

'Oh, Bess, don't say such things. I am trying very hard to convince myself that I could grow to like Sir Edward once I know him.'

The tears now blurring her vision refused to be kept at bay.

'There, there, my pet,' Bess soothed, wrapping her arms round Jane and holding her tightly.

She crooned a lullaby as she smoothed the hair back from Jane's beautiful forehead, until the girl had quietened down.

'The other day when that strange woman, Jedaan, came into the garden, do you remember what she told me, Bess? She said that he whose bride I would be would not be of my father's choosing.'

'Aye, pet, but you can't believe in such things,' Bess said kindly.

Both women remained silent for a time then Jane moved over to the window.

'I wonder if Master Fornton is very badly wounded, Bess.'

'We'll find out soon, my pet. I've sent Syd Dawson to the inn at Rowton and he will bring us back the news.'

Syd Dawson was well known in Rowton and found no lack of people to give their various accounts of the story. The landlord gave him such a lugubrious account of the condition of his guest and protested so bitterly that the wounded man should not be disturbed that Dawson felt that there was no longer any ground to hope that Master Fornton would live.

The reports were at first fatalistic, but over a few days they changed, recounting how the gentleman was recovering well without the skills of a surgeon. Bess was able to convey the news to Jane who received it with a combination of relief and curiosity, particularly when she learned of Jedaan's involvement.

Jane was not the only one to be curious. As John continued to improve,

Jedaan's skills as a quack doctor gave her status amongst the village community to whom she was an object of intense curiosity mingled with awe. She turned her remedial knowledge to profitable account telling fortunes and selling charms, making tisanes for fever and selling cures for toothache.

'I must leave here soon, Jedaan,' John informed her as she treated his wound one day. 'My sister is fretting. She insists that I go to Migfield Manor as soon as I am able to travel. It is only ten miles away. When do you think I will be strong enough to make the journey?'

After all she had done for him, John would never disclose to Jedaan that his sister was trying to assert her authority by not only demanding he recuperate at her home but also put himself in the hands of her own trusted surgeon instead of some wild woman.

'I can't agree to any travel. You are much too weak,' Jedaan assured him. 'Any excess movement would undo all the good work.'

John was too grateful to argue and now that he was convinced that no vital organ was injured, he had the utmost confidence in her truly remarkable skills. She rewarded this confidence with her unremitting attention and after a week allowed him to get up and sit in the autumn sunshine with his arm bound carefully to his side in case any movement should again start the bleeding.

Here he sat under a spreading tree chatting with the village folk. He began to feel quite an attachment to these people who certainly helped to relieve the monotony of his enforced confinement. Syd Dawson found him there one day when he called at the hostelry, and although he had never met the young man, he was well aware that this was the same John Fornton about whom he had been sent by Bess to enquire. He made an obeisance to John, who readily entered into conversation with him.

When he learned that he was head

forester to Sir George Holdenate, John's interest grew. Dawson was an intelligent fellow and informed his willing listener that his father and his grandfather before him had been in the Holdenate's service and he himself had served the family for forty years.

'Then you have seen a good many changes,' John suggested with interest.

'Aye, sir, that I have. I remember my lady, who died sadly, coming to the Hall as a bride, and the joy when Mistress Jane was born. And then the death of my dear lady earlier this year. That was a sore time, sir.'

Syd shook his head in a perplexed manner.

'Begging your leniency if I seem too bold of speech, sir, but she would never have entertained the likes of Sir Edward. He may have a title, but he is no gentleman. He would never have been welcome here when my lady was alive and now he is betrothed to one I would shed my heart's blood for. It's

114

not for me to say aught against my betters, but he has an evil reputation, a hasty temper and a rough tongue.'

'To which I can bear testimony,' John smirked, rubbing his hand over his bound arm. 'Give me your hand, Syd Dawson. You are an honest fellow and I like you.'

As he spoke, John offered his ringed hand to the woodsman who stared at him in surprise.

'But, sir, my hand is rough and course for the work I do is hard.'

'Well, what does that matter? Give me your hand, man.'

Honest Syd Dawson was confused and agitated by having his hand shaken by this gentleman of quality, this son of an earl. His bewilderment deprived him of speech yet his expression conveyed a wealth of high esteem. Eventually he found his voice.

'Sir, I am your humble servant, at your service. If you would deign to entrust me with any message to be delivered to Ladsill Hall, it will be truly and secretly given, or may God forget me.'

'A thousand thanks, but I am a stranger to Ladsill Hall. Why should I send messages?'

'I know not, sir,' Syd stated looking slightly confused.

Of course John Fornton was entirely ignorant of the extraordinary interest that old Bess had taken in his welfare, sending Syd to gain information, as he now realised.

'Then if you would pardon my freedom of speech,' Syd stated thinking fast, 'I thought you would command me to bespeak you well to my mistress through old Bess, her tire woman.'

John evinced surprise as he rose from his seat and looked into the other man's face.

'Do you think that Lady Jane has heard of my encounter with Sir Edward Sutton?'

'Do I think so, sir? Nay, I dare be sworn. Why 'tis common talk everywhere hereabouts.'

'In that case, if you should happen to speak with Bess soon, say you have talked with the gentleman who was wounded and that he prays for God's blessings upon her mistress. You need say no more.'

' 'Tis a good message, sir, and I will give it. 'Twill go to my lady's heart for she is of great tenderness.'

John smiled, heaved a heavy sigh and turned away as Dawson mounted his horse ready to leave.

'By the saints, I swear I will also tell her that thou dids't sigh as if thine own heart were bursting with love for her,' Dawson beamed urging his horse forward.

John swung round to correct him, but Dawson had dug his heels into the mare's side and was galloping away as John's words of denial hung in empty air. He ground his heel angrily on the gravel and cursed himself for being so open.

Would to God I had never seen her, he thought angrily to himself, yet, would to God my sword had found the heart of Sir Edward Sutton. If fortune would give me another chance I warrant my hand would not lose its cunning again, and Lady Jane would be saved for a better man.

BANKSTOWN
LIBRARY & KNOWLEDGE CENTRE

Receipt

Returned items

1. Danger comes calling /   returned
   Karen Abbott

2. Shade of happiness / Karen   returned
   Abbott

3. Summer Island / Karen   returned
   Abbott

4.   returned

14/01/2022 10:01:12

Hours
Mon-Fri 9am-6pm
Sat 9am-4pm
Sun 1pm-4pm

1. Taking ~~over~~
2. Mistress of Her Fate
   The Love that's
3. Heals

5

Surely there would be no harm in visiting Master Fornton now he is recovered!' Jane cried in exasperation. 'You told me yourself he sits most days under the chestnut tree in front of the inn. Please, Bess, I need to know what was said to provoke a duel and if Master Fornton knows something about Sir Edward that could sway my father against this betrothal.'

Old Bess continued to insist it was not correct for a young lady to visit a gentleman! She shook her head, determined to resist any persuasion by her young mistress although they both knew she was weakening.

'Then why not send one of the servants you can trust and arrange that we meet Master Fornton while we are out riding here on the Ladsill estate? If anyone should see us, it would seem like an innocent meeting. You must help me, Bess, please.'

The pleading, coupled with this new angle was too much for Bess who nodded slowly.

'I'll do what I can but don't expect too much. Master Fornton is a gentleman and I dare say he'd rather tear out his tongue than tell you aught against your intended.'

Syd Dawson was only too happy to deliver Bess's message but John's initial reaction of surprise and delight was followed by a feeling of suspicion. Was this a genuine assignation on the part of Bess, or some deep-laid scheme against his honour or his safety, possibly a trap to draw him into a fresh quarrel? Yet, if not, why should Bess have sent him such a request? Assuming that she had, was it likely she would have made known her intention to her mistress and might Lady Jane have favoured the idea?

The following day a searching wind blew along the valley, tossing the branches of the trees about with a meaningless fury, and raising clouds of dust. The sky was heavy and there were signs that foretold rain. Naturally, this was not conducive to John's mood for if rain fell, it was hardly to be expected that Lady Jane would ride in the woods. He watched the lowering sky and listened to the fiendish screech of the wind as he dismissed his bewildered servant and rode away alone.

He pulled his hat down farther as big, intermittent drops of rain proclaimed the coming storm. He travelled on, of necessity taking the highway past The Peacock then up through the meadow, and into the forest. He did not hurry. In such wind and rain Lady Jane would not venture out. She would be snugly housed beneath Ladsill's sheltering roof, giving no thought to the foolish gentleman who was ploughing his way over the wet and mossy track in the vain hope of seeing her.

A rustic hut, built of gnarled branches and thatched deeply with straw, stood melancholy in the gloom of the forest. This was the meeting place yet, at a distance, John could see no sign of life. He would go as far as the hut, check, then hurry back. There was no need to linger, even though it was not yet the appointed hour of noon. They wouldn't come, not in this weather.

He dismounted and labouring forward with these thoughts in mind, a sound reached his ears. It was a voice, a woman's voice. He paused to listen then gasped in bewilderment. He hurried forward and as he rounded the hut, his eyes rested on Jane and Bess, sheltering beneath the porch.

'Master Fornton,' Bess stated with feigned surprise in her voice. 'What brings you here on such a day?'

'It was kind fate that led me,' John replied as he bowed courteously.

Jane nodded in greeting and a smile tilted the corners of her full lips. She wore a riding cloak of silver grey with a hood that came up over her head, framing her beautiful face. She appeared to John's enraptured gaze like a saint which the hand and genius of an artist had caught and placed on canvas.

'It is strange that you should come at this time when Bess and I were driven here for shelter against this persistent rain,' Jane said twisting her riding crop nervously between gloved fingers and hoping the lie wasn't too apparent. 'It has, however, given me the opportunity of enquiring about your health, sir.'

'Many thanks for your interest, my lady. I am extremely well.'

'Yet I heard you had a distressing wound.'

All Jane's nervousness had now gone.

'It was but a scratch,' he replied.

'Then have the gossips lied? It was said that you were sick unto death.'

'Death has passed me by and taken better men,' John replied, suitably rebuked.

'Then God has spared you for better fortune, Master Fornton, but I would like to hear from your own lips the cause of the quarrel.'

'Words, my lady, words,' he answered with a smile, 'and yet words of grave offence lightly spoken.'

'Against Sir Edward Sutton?' Jane asked anxiously.

'Yes, against Sir Edward Sutton,' John admitted reluctantly.

'Then tell me, Master Fornton,' she asked with a strange, eager earnestness, 'and tell me truly, do you know aught of evil against Sir Edward?'

A pitiable look of despair swept across John's handsome face as this question placed him in an exceedingly awkward position. Here was an affianced bride asking him if he knew anything evil of her husband-elect. A man of less scruples could have turned the situation to his advantage by trying to disgrace Sir Edward, yet John was reluctant to do so.

'Lady Jane, Sir Edward Sutton and I have crossed swords and a young gentleman has been slain because in idle moments I spoke some ill-considered words.'

'Master Fornton,' Jane stated in a stern tone, 'you are juggling with the truth. If your words were without warrant, then you were guilty of a most wicked act. If, on the contrary, there was justification for your words, I am deeply interested to know.'

John placed his hand upon his heart and looked into her searching eyes with an honest, unwavering gaze.

'My lady, I know nothing from personal knowledge of Sir Edward Sutton.'

'Master Fornton,' Jane stated almost as solemnly, 'the story runs that you uttered words against Sir Edward. I am sure that you would not speak of matters without fair warrant so now, sir, I beseech you to tell me what those words were.'

'But Sir Edward is to be your lord,' John stammered.

'That does not matter,' she replied

hotly. 'Please give me the information I seek.'

John's confusion increased as, dragging his eyes away from her pleading look, he realised that Bess had slipped away.

'You appeal to my honour, lady, and I yield,' John said helplessly. 'I have heard it said many times that Sir Edward is a dicer and a man of loose habits. He has been in many broils due to his unhappy temper and has been known to speak lightly of many fair women. These matters are common talk and when a man's reputation is attacked by many, it is to be accepted that at least a few speak truly.'

John paused and looked enquiringly at Jane whose face had now lost its outward calm.

'I had no wish to upset you, my lady. I spoke of this only because you wished me to do so,' John stated apologetically as Jane shuddered.

'Master Fornton, I thank you for telling me,' she stammered in a voice that spoke plainly of struggling emotions. 'Why is my father not aware of this? Would you . . . no, I couldn't ask.'

'Ask me anything and I would be honoured to do whatever is in my power to do. I am your servant, always, Lady Jane.'

Jane turned away and began to pace the confined space as John stood helplessly watching. Suddenly she stopped as if her mind was made up. She turned to him.

'Would you make this information known to my father?' she asked.

'Mistress, I hardly know your father. It would be highly irregular for me to approach him with these words. Sir Edward has found favour in his eyes or why else would he have agreed to your betrothal?'

'My father's only wish is to find me a husband who will protect me and my property when anything happens to him. He wants to be sure I will be taken care of.'

'Lady Jane, that is an honour every

red-blooded man in the kingdom would die for.'

'Why do you mock me, Master Fornton? I have unburdened myself to you and yet now I see you treat my words very lightly.'

John stepped forward, propelled by an overwhelming need to take her into his arms, yet Jane covered her face with her hands in a gesture of horrified confusion.

'Lady Jane, believe me, I do not take your words lightly. I speak from my heart when I tell you that I would willingly lay down my life for you.'

As he spoke, his hands cupped her elbows and slowly she lowered her hands to stare at him in bewilderment. Their eyes held for a long moment then she looked away in embarrassment.

'If you were not betrothed, I would be speaking to your father on a very different matter.'

'And what would that be, Master Fornton?' Jane asked, her curiosity now outweighing propriety.

'Protocol would dictate that I must speak to him before making my feelings known to you, my lady.'

'Your feelings, sir? Are you feeling sorry for me?'

'I am feeling sorry for myself.'

'What does that mean?'

It was now John's turn to look away in confusion yet she watched him with impatience, fearing that they may be disturbed at any moment and she would never learn what he was reluctant to say.

'Should I feel sorry for you, Master Fornton?' she teased trying to lighten the mood.

'I would be interested to know what feelings you hold for me, Lady Jane,' he replied levelly.

'How can I answer such a question when I hardly know you,' she said, giving him a coy look.

'I hardly know you, yet I knew the first moment I set eyes on you that you were special. You are the lady I've been searching for, and I find you just as you are pledged to another, to my great sorrow.'

John paused and took a deep breath.

'Now do you perhaps feel sorry for me?' he ended.

The silence was electric as they looked at each other then John moved forward slowly and took her gently into his arms.

'This is madness, I know, yet I can't help myself. If your father was to find out, or Sir Edward, I would no doubt be following poor Sir Ralph to an early grave.'

'Please, don't jest about such things,' Jane whispered giving an involuntary shiver which prompted John to hold her closer.

She gave no resistance as he tilted her face to his and looked into her eyes. She had never been so close to another person before yet felt no revulsion or dislike, in fact the strange sensations that were coursing through her body were inexplicable, unexpected and exciting. She remembered that day in the garden when he had caught her in his arms and kissed her. Then, protocol dictated that she should show anger towards him but now, if he were to kiss her, she might respond.

'Could you perhaps learn to like me a little?' he asked slowly, his eyes burning deep into her soul.

'I already like you a lot, Master Fornton,' she replied boldly.

'As much as your intended lord?' he asked breaking the magic as her eyes glazed over with dread.

'My feelings for Sir Edward are all sour. There is no warmth nor love between us. Surely you can't think I would be here in your arms if I had any feelings for him.'

She let out a choked sob and pulled away as Bess, appearing from nowhere, hurried forward and caught her in her arms.

'What does this mean?' she demanded glaring at John. 'Have you insulted my sweet child? You will pay dearly if so.'

131

'Good nurse, your devotion to your ward does you credit but I can assure you I would never knowingly insult your lady,' John protested giving Bess a pained look. 'I hold her in much too high regard.'

Jane composed herself with difficulty as she traced a slender finger across her cheek bone, wiping away a stray tear.

'Master Fornton, you are a gentleman and I thank you for being honest with me.'

She held out her hand and John dropped to one knee, seizing her hand and pressing it gently to his lips.

'I am your humble servant, Lady Jane,' he said, pulling himself from his knees yet reluctant to release her hand.

'Forgive me, my lady,' old Bess faltered, 'and you, fair sir, forgive me but we must get homeward. The rain has ceased but I doubt if it will hold for long. The horses are getting restless to be in drier conditions.'

The two ladies prepared to leave and as John helped Jane into her saddle she whispered a reassurance of her thanks as she bade him farewell. The warmth of her gaze held him mesmerised and he stared after the departing figures long after they had been swallowed up by the forest. He was alone and the rain was falling again but he was in a much lighter mood as he retraced his steps.

The following day, Jane was informed that her father was asking for her and as the request seemed laced with urgency, she hurried to find him. A glance at her father's stern face did nothing to reassure her.

'I have just entertained Master John Fornton,' he informed her and was amazed to see her eyes light up at the mention of his name.

'I had no idea he was here,' Jane replied wanting to excuse herself to go in search of him. 'Will he be staying long?'

'He has left already.'

'Left?' Jane echoed. 'But I haven't seen him.'

'I wasn't aware that you were

interested in seeing my messengers, Jane!'

'No, Father,' Jane said, her voice small and faltering. 'But surely Master Fornton is not merely a messenger.'

'Why do you say that? Would I be correct in thinking that Master Fornton has found favour in your eyes?'

Jane blushed most charmingly.

'I would like to get to know him better, Father.'

'Which is a more positive sentiment than you have expressed towards Sir Edward. Could it be that Master Fornton has wormed his way into your affections? Knowing you are the bride to be of Sir Edward, that is a most ungentlemanly thing to do. I was obviously correct in sending him away.'

'You sent him away? But, why? Did he say aught to displease you?'

'He asked that I should consider him a suitable suitor for your hand. I ask you, Jane, why should a man ask for your hand when it is common knowledge that you are betrothed to another?'

Jane stared at her father with blind eyes. John had asked for her hand! He wanted to marry her.

'What was your reply, Father?' Jane mumbled, almost afraid to ask.

'What do you think? Even if he was the King himself, I am not a man to go back on my word. You will marry Sir Edward and promise me never to see John Fornton again.'

Jane uttered a choked sob.

'But, Father, I could never, ever love Sir Edward, particularly now. Didn't Master Fornton tell you anything about Sir Edward, about his character, his morals, his reputation?'

'Why should a man like Fornton tell me things about your intended lord unless he was intent upon discrediting him in some way?' he asked logically. 'If Master Fornton had tried to influence me by speaking of such things it would not have gone in his favour.'

'Then if I were to tell you, would you think less of me?'

'Nay, my child. You are only the

mouthpiece for another. You have said yourself you hardly know Sir Edward. Put these thoughts out of your mind and when Sir Edward arrives, as he is expected to do in a few days time, make yourself agreeable to him.'

Jane gave her father one agonised look, excused herself and ran from the room where Bess was waiting to console her. She pressed a tightly-folded letter into Jane's hand and as she looked at it in amazement, she realised it must be from John. Gaining the security of her own chamber, she tore open the letter and began to read.

My dearest Lady Jane,

I have been unable to get you out of my mind and after our meeting yesterday I knew I couldn't stand back and see you married to a man you did not love. I must try to warn your father of Sir Edward's reputation although I'm sure he will think the worse of me for doing so. I intend to make my feelings for you known to your father and ask for your hand.

My dearest love, if he agrees, you will never see this letter, but as I have a disquieting feeling that things may not go well I want you to know you are forever in my thoughts.

Your obedient servant
John Fornton.

★　★　★

Sir Edward returned from Cheshire in anything but a pleasant frame of mind. The relatives of his late young friend held him morally responsible for the boy's death, so it was not surprising that he had left Cheshire under a cloud. But he was a reckless man who would not allow the death of an insignificant youth to interfere with his schemes. Firstly, he must cement his union with Lady Jane. That would not only bring him great wealth, but more power, and the thought pleased him immensely.

Short though his visit to Ladsill Hall was, he found time to call into The

Peacock Inn on the Ladsill estate where Hubert Armstrong lost no time in imparting the news that John Fornton had been seen lingering in the neighbourhood and rumours hinted that the reason was Lady Jane.

Later, at Ladsill Hall, making profuse apologies for the briefness of his visit, Sir Edward voiced his view that an early date should be set for the wedding. Sir George nodded his agreement, but much to Jane's relief, he made no move to name the day.

The following morning, Sir Edward left the area and although Jane was not interested in the urgency of his departure, she was greatly relieved to see him go. The following day, Bess informed her that John Fornton had left the area, too, and a dreadful thought tortured Jane. Perhaps Sir Edward had killed him. Jane ordered Bess to find out more and later Bess returned with fragments of news.

'The landlord of the inn at Rowton confirmed that John Fornton left in a hurry,' Bess stated, 'and no-one seems to know the whereabouts of Sir Edward but if anything is amiss, we will hear soon enough.'

'Did Master Fornton leave alone?' Jane questioned excitedly.

'I believe so,' Bess stammered giving her a sidelong look. 'But that doesn't mean he didn't meet up with someone later.'

Jane was suddenly aware that Bess seemed ill at ease and unwilling to continue.

'Is this someone other than Sir Edward?' she asked carefully, watching Bess closely. 'Do you know something I should possibly know, Bess?'

'Not really, my lady. I only tell you this 'cause it has found most credence with the rustics. They say that he has absconded.'

'What? John Fornton has stolen something and run away in order to avoid prosecution? That's ridiculous. What is he supposed to have stolen?'

'Probably absconded is not quite the

right word. He's eloped, my lady.'

'Eloped! With whom? Jedaan, the gipsy?' Jane laughed. 'This story is preposterous.'

'Aye, my lady, yet is it just coincidence that Mary Armstrong, the daughter of Hubert Armstrong, landlord of The Peacock, has gone, too? Disappeared without a word she has.'

Bess paused for a moment before continuing.

'There is nobody who can say that John Fornton and the fair Mary have been seen together but rumour says that Master John went to a secret meeting with her only this week. The weather was foul and he was in a stormy mood, yet according to the ostler, when he returned, his mood was changed completely and he paid the ostler a silver groat. Something pleasant had happened in that time to make him change his mood.'

'How does this imply that Mary Armstrong was involved?' Jane questioned.

'He was seen passing The Peacock and there would appear to be no other reason for him to be in that area.'

'That means nothing,' Jane stated angrily. 'Why should people make up that kind of story? Are these folks always ready with venom on their tongues?'

'It's her reputation, my pet. Mary is a pretty wench but has a reputation as being flighty. She trifles with this lad and flirts with that one and many a village swain has broken his heart over her. But Mary is ambitious and no doubt the glamour of an earl's son was too tempting for her to turn down.

'Some say that's why her father told Sir Edward what John Fornton had said about him. It was his way of getting even. Now she has gone and John Fornton has gone, too. What could be more certain than that they have gone together? It's a fine piece of rustic logic that counts for little, but to certain shallow minds, the fact remains that they are both away and that counts for much.'

'No, I can't accept that. He wouldn't say the things he did to me or come here and ask my father for my hand in marriage. Why would he send me that note if all the time he was planning to take Mary Armstrong away? I can't believe it for a moment. There must be someone who knows where he has gone. Can you send someone to Rowton to see if he told anyone where he was heading?'

'I'll see if Syd Dawson can find out any more. He'll know whom to ask, but I'm sure he's already questioned them. I'll just say this, my pet. Since we are discussing what might have happened, might it not be that Sir Edward has taken the maid away?'

'Oh, Bess!' Jane gasped, the paleness of her face glowing with a sudden flush of excitement. 'If Sir Edward has taken Mary with or without the girl's full consent, my father would call off our betrothal, wouldn't he?'

'Aye, he probably would, my pet, but proof would be demanded and we have no proof. It is not for me to speak with certainty when I have no warrant, but I believe Sir Edward is loose enough for any wickedness.'

6

The moors grew white with the first dusting of winter snow before Jane received a message from John, and although it was brief, it was enough to reassure her that his feelings for her had not changed. Bess, who had delivered the message, watched her read then gave a toothless smile as she saw the happiness radiating from her charge.

'He is well, but didn't say where he is,' she informed Bess as she slowly put down the letter. 'Did the messenger say anything?'

'Only to make sure this went directly to your hands. Would you like to question him further? He has been partaking of some food so he'll either be in the kitchen or in the courtyard now. Shall we go and see?'

Jane was already reaching for her cloak and as Bess followed her example, the two ladies made their way down-stairs. There was no sign of the messenger in the great, hot, steamy kitchens where a huge amount of preparation was underway in readiness for the Christmas festivities.

They made their way outside and Bess indicated the messenger standing by the side of the still-room wall. He had his back turned to the two ladies, yet even as she looked, Jane felt a strange awareness. A second later, he turned and Jane knew instantly, despite the beard and hat pulled low over his face, that this was John Fornton himself!

'My lady,' he said removing his hat and giving a low bow. 'I trust the message was well received.'

'Indeed it was, sir, yet how am I able to answer it when I have no indication where to forward my reply?'

'If there is a reply, you can relate it to me now and I can assure you it will be gratefully received,' he said slowly, his eyes holding hers.

As they spoke, Bess scanned the area and once she was satisfied all was clear, she hastened Jane and John into the fragrant still-room which thankfully was empty. With her faithful nurse on guard, Jane hesitated for only a second before going into his arms.

'My dearest love,' he whispered nuzzling into her silky hair. 'I had to see you and knew that your father would forbid me. Did Bess tell you I was here?'

Jane lifted her head in surprise.

'Bess informed me of the messenger. I think she probably didn't recognise you with a beard.'

'Nay, your good nurse and Syd Dawson made this meeting possible. The beard is a safeguard in case your father or any of the house guests should see me.'

Jane laughed quietly.

'I like it, but why did you take such a chance?'

'To see you, my love. I've heard no news of your wedding plans yet

146

dared not hope your father had cancelled them. Is Sir Edward still your intended?'

'I regret to say he is, although he is not the one in my heart, my lord.'

As she spoke, John's arms tightened around her and his lips moved gently over hers as he kissed her tenderly. Her trembling body responded as she returned his kiss, clinging to him as if she couldn't bear to let him go. Eventually he lifted his head and gazed into her eyes.

'I can't just accept that you are to marry that man. I will not let you. I'm on my way to Lancashire now and I will not return until I've found some proof that will show Sir Edward in his true light. Then your father will have to reconsider.'

'Be careful, my love. Sir Edward is cruel and spiteful. He will not take kindly to you prying around in his home county.'

'That is why I am going now. The Christmas festivities are beginning and he will be away. I understand he will be here for several days.'

'Your informant has done a thorough job. Yes, Sir Edward and his family are due to arrive in a few days. The thought of entertaining them over Christmas has given me no pleasure, but now I have hope.'

'And I need your assurance that you will not encourage the advances of Sir Edward while I'm away,' he joked as Jane gave a low moan. 'I will return in ten days time and if all has gone to plan, that will be the last you need see of Sir Edward Sutton.'

'This is like a dream,' she whispered as he kissed her lightly. 'No, it is better than a dream. You are here and I can't believe it.'

'The next time we meet, we can show our love in the open, then this will all seem like some dreadful nightmare. Until then my love.'

With a long, lingering kiss they parted and as Bess signalled the way was clear, John strode off to his horse while Bess and Jane hurried back upstairs. She had previously dreaded the thought of having the attentions of Sir Edward throughout the Christmas festivities yet, as her intended, it would have appeared highly irregular not to have invited him, his mother and three sisters. Her father had pointed out the necessity of meeting his family, yet to Jane it was just another step nearer to their intended nuptials. Now she had fresh hope.

When they arrived, she greeted Sir Edward with cool indifference then her eyes rested on Lady Sutton, a bloated lady with excessive amounts of spare flesh on her bones. The two exchanged greetings with no hint of warmth and Jane gave a deep curtsey out of respect to the middle-aged matron.

'You are not what I expected at all,' Lady Sutton stated, piercing Jane with her sharp grey eyes. 'Pretty enough, I dare say, but you obviously lack a mother's guiding hand. Goodness me, when I was your age — but when you are married . . . '

Her voice trailed away as Jane closed her mind to any further conversation, biting her lower lip hard in an attempt to maintain control. How could Lady Sutton be so insensitive knowing that her dear mother had so recently died? Jane wanted to escape, but knew that that would be impossible, so instead, she scrutinised the dictatorial ogress and tried to imagine Lady Sutton at her age. One look at the assorted shapes and sizes of her daughters gave no clue, as they in turn eyes Jane with haughty disdain.

Feeling overpowered and oppressed by their very presence Jane left the Sutton party at the first opportunity and vowed to avoid them in future at all cost. Thankfully there were too many other guests for them to expect their hostess's personal attention and Jane found it easiest to hide her contempt thinly disguised beneath a veneer of assumed cordiality. Lady Sutton, after her initial attempts at domination, found others to form her circle, who were much more eager to hang on her every word.

Merriment punctuated by feasting continued for four days, yet Lady Sutton still grumbled about all the negative aspects of the visit. Alongside groups of musicians, a professional company of actors had been hired by Sir George, though Lady Sutton voiced her opinion that plays were drawing apprentices away from their regular employment, and casting young boys in female rôles was nothing short of immoral.

On the final evening, a jousting tournament was held by torchlight and as a grand finale, a fireworks display of blazing darts, flights of thunderbolts, rays of glistening stars and streams of fiery hail and sparks could be heard and seen with amazement twenty miles away. Much later, Jane climbed into bed exhausted and snuggled into her feather mattress. The muffled thud of the door closing disturbed her and sleepily she wondered why Bess had entered her chamber at this time of night. Then she heard the shuffle of heavy feet and knew that this was not Bess.

She lay motionless, her eyes now open wide to the darkness, lit only by the low burning embers in the grate. The silence was weighty with expectation, broken only by heavy breathing and the thunderous pounding of her own heart. She wanted to cry out, to alert Bess, yet what if this person had genuinely made a wrong choice of room? He would soon realise and beat a hasty retreat. It would only lead to confusion and embarrassment if she were to make any moves. She lay rigidly trying to keep calm as the footsteps grew nearer then stopped.

Slowly she lowered the bed cover and peered at the intruder whose figure was silhouetted against the glow of the fire. Even though she could not see his face there was no mistaking the huge, padded frame of Sir Edward Sutton.

She gazed at him with terror in her eyes as he swayed a little, then raised a silver goblet to his lips. She heard the sound of the remainder of the wine being gulped down, then the goblet being thrown to the floor.

He took another step closer, then another. She wanted to scream but her whole body was paralysed with fear. An instant later, he was by her bed, pulling her to her feet. In an instant, his arms held her in a vice-like grip and her scream was silenced by his lips cold, wet and hard covering hers, crushing them brutally. She squirmed, trying desperately to free herself. This just seemed to be arousing him more. She forced her lips open to scream only to find his mouth again pressing on hers. She was frightened, disgusted and appalled. Panic and sickness rose up inside her as she realised the enormity of what he might do and just how helpless she was to prevent it. With one colossal effort, she wrenched her lips away and screamed, but the sound was feeble and thin.

'What's the matter, mistress? You can't deny your intended lord,' he slurred.

'You are drunk, sir.'

'Only drunk for you. You flaunt and tempt and say you will be my wife, but when? How much longer do I have to wait? This could be our wedding night then I would not have to endure such provocation a moment longer. Come, wench, I will show you.'

His words stopped mid-sentence as his great bulk toppled forward and rolled on to the floor. Behind where he had just been standing, a diminutive Bess in her night attire still held an enormous log selected quickly from the basket by the fire. Jane sank down on to the bed and Bess rushed forward to hold her trembling form.

'It's all right now, my pet, it's all right,' she assured her.

'Oh, Bess, I can't believe it.'

Jane sobbed noisily, clinging to Bess.

'He tried to force himself upon me and if you hadn't arrived when you did he . . . '

Jane collapsed in tears. Bess tried to comfort her charge while trying to work out in her own simple fashion what to do next. No way would she have the reputation of her sweet one besmirched by some lustful man with no morals and even less conscience.

If Sir George was to find out, honour would decree that he would challenge Sir Edward, but as Sir Edward had proved, he was a first-class swordsman who would in any conflict, inflict injury, if not death, on his opponent. Sir George, being much slower and older would not stand a chance. Bess could not risk that happening. She had to think of an alternative and fast.

He could be stirring any moment and then what? Suddenly Bess felt herself go rigid. What if she had killed him? She would hang for this! Oh, mercy! Well, if she were going to hang, she would make sure beforehand that her darling's reputation was intact. The body must be moved.

'Jane, my pet,' she whispered, giving Jane's limp body a firm shake as she wrapped her shawl tightly round her. 'We need to remove him, quickly.'

Without a word, Jane stood up, pulled the table carpet from the coffer and spread it out by the side of Sir Edward. Together they rolled the bulky frame on to the carpet and, in uneven jerks, pulled it towards the door.

'We'll never get him away from here,' Bess puffed, being unfamiliar with such strenuous exertion as she collapsed on to a stool.

'Of course, we will. Come, Bess. I will open the door into the corridor and if it is clear we must drag him as far as we can, then roll him off the carpet and return here.'

Bess took two more good breaths and Jane furtively opened the door and peered out. All was clear. The door was flung open and together they pulled and pulled until they reached the top of the stairs. A quick exchange of looks confirmed their joint decision and with one jubilant push, the body of Sir Edward tumbled awkwardly down the stairs to land in a heap at the bottom. As it came to rest, an audible gasp escaped it and Bess opened wide eyes.

'He's still alive, the sluggard,' Bess exclaimed with a mixture of relief and wonder. 'I thought I had killed him,' she confessed, 'although after what he did to you, my pet, he deserves to die.'

Dragging the carpet behind them, they returned hastily to Jane's chamber and listened for any further developments, but all was silent as the household slept. Bess firmly locked the door and tucked Jane up in bed before making up a truckle bed for herself for the night. Jane remained silent but slowly Bess detected from her breathing pattern that at last she was asleep. She tiptoed over to check.

'Have no fear, little one,' she whispered silently looking down at her beautiful charge. 'While old Bess is here, nothing will harm thee.'

Next morning, Bess woke to find Jane, her head bowed in grief, weeping bitterly. Bess hurried to comfort her and alarmed by her burning face and blood-shot eyes, she instructed rest and a hot posset but Jane needed reassurance.

'Sir Edward, is there any news?' she stammered.

'He's not dead if that's what you mean and I think your father will make sure he returns home today, fit or not.'

'Has my father said anything? Does he suspect anything?' she mumbled bashfully.

Bess shook her head.

'He suspects nothing and I hardly think Sir Edward is likely to do the decent thing and confess, do you?'

'He would never throw himself at my father's mercy but . . . ' Jane's voice trailed away in embarrassment. 'What if he were to approach my father and threaten to besmirch my honour, slander my name?'

'Trouble yourself not, my pet. Even Sir Edward would not stoop to those depths. Your father is far too powerful a man and makes a better ally than enemy. Sir Edward and his family have shown themselves in their true colours this time, even your father can't have failed to notice. But he's a proud man and one who does not like to be proved wrong. Just wait until Master Fornton returns then things will change.'

'Dear God, I hope you are right, Bess. I could not live with the shame. I would rather die than face Sir Edward again now.'

Bess informed Sir George that Jane was not well and must be excused from the duty of exchanging courteous goodbyes with all their guests. Sir George, delighted at the success of the holiday festivities and the excellent way his young daughter had coped, accepted this as he went through the duty of seeing off his guests alone.

Sir Edward was born off in a litter, much to his humiliation and the general amusement of the other guests, after supposedly suffering a mysterious fall the previous evening. An astute observer would have detected the lack of eye contact between Sir George and Sir Edward and the general coolness shown as the Sutton party left Ladsill Hall.

Now Jane waited eagerly for the arrival of John Fornton but as January's blanket of snow and unusually hard frosts crept into February without news of him, she began to worry. The rutted highways, now frost hardened, made travel almost impossible but with the thaw, fords swelled by melted snow turned the highways into rivers of mud.

Jane had a feeling of unease but the only person she could confide in was Bess who continued to assure her that all would be well in due course. With the first signs of spring, a messenger arrived and although Jane was delighted to at last have news of John, her disappointment at not seeing him personally was like a physical blow.

'Why couldn't he come as a messenger like he did last time?' Jane asked Bess as they hurried to the privacy of Jane's chamber.

'You know he took a great risk that day, my pet. If your father had seen him, or worse still, seen you together, he would have refused him the hospitality of Ladsill, permanently.'

'I see no difference. As far as my father is concerned, John has been banned from Ladsill after voicing his wish to marry me.'

As she spoke, she settled down to read and Bess remained silent, watching Jane's changing expressions. At last she lowered the pages and looked at Bess, a look of anguish painting her face.

'I must go to him, Bess. He's injured and it's all my fault.'

Jane burst into tears and Bess hurried forward to comfort her.

'What does the letter say?' Bess asked.

Jane dabbed her eyes, gave a noisy sniff and began.

'Master Fornton has returned to Migfield Manor,' she said then read from the letter. 'My stay at the local hostelry on Sir Edward's estate didn't go unnoticed but I kept myself to myself while I made discreet enquiries. I followed every lead yet always drew a blank. Every time I thought I had found someone who was willing to talk, they either changed their mind or disappeared. Finally I had a midnight visit from two ruffians and I'd rather gloss over what they said and did. Suffice to say I couldn't get up for some days after their visit. The good thing is, I recognised one as the esquire who had been present at the duel at Rowton so I knew they were obviously Sutton's henchmen acting on his orders.'

'That is shocking!' Bess declared with a surge of anger. 'Poor Master Fornton. I hope he didn't suffer too much. I know you want to go to him but it would not be proper. I could send Syd Dawson to Migfield Manor to enquire as to Master Fornton's health, then perhaps you might get an invitation from his sister, Lady Talbot. Maybe he doesn't want you to know the full extent of his injuries for fear of worrying you.'

'I will worry whichever way. I feel responsible. If only he hadn't gone. I fear that he has aggravated the situation and with the roads now passable Sir Edward can be expected to arrive any day. Oh, Bess, this is like some dreadful nightmare. I see Sir Edward looming larger and larger and John Fornton growing smaller and smaller. Oh, what's to be done?'

Bess shook her head solemnly. She, too, felt miserable and downhearted for she had held such faith in John Fornton. She had believed that he of all people could find something or someone to confirm once and for all that Sir Edward Sutton was rotten through and through, yet now her hopes were dashed.

'I will write to John, suggested he comes and informs my father of this cruel turn of events. Tell Syd Dawson to be ready to leave within the hour and not to return until he has learned the full extent of John's injuries.'

Syd Dawson returned the following day, not only with news of Master Fornton but some local gossip that he felt would be of interest to Bess. Mary Armstrong had returned home heavy with child and been thrown out by her father. No-one knew where she had been, but it was obvious what she had been up to. Syd may have been surprised yet showed no emotions when Bess informed him that Lady Jane wished to make contact with Mary as soon as possible.

Mary Armstrong, sheltered from the worse of the elements in a woodsman's barn, the other side of Lectonfield, gave birth to a baby boy and although the girl was physically exhausted and suffering from lack of food, the baby was fine and healthy. The woodsman's wife took care of the girl and the new arrival. Her husband would have turned the girl out, but the two groats given him by the gentleman when he brought Mary to them, had bought him plenty of ale and with a possibility of the aristocrat returning and giving him more, it was beneficial for him to allow her to stay.

His new-found wealth did not go unnoticed at the local ale house and soon the tale of the homeless girl and her new-born infant reached the ears of Syd Dawson who was able to impart the knowledge and the whereabouts to Bess. She and Lady Jane had no difficulty in finding the woodsman's house and much to the astonishment of his wife, appeared in the yard.

Jane asked to see the girl and was shown into the dimly-lit stable. Mary stared at the visitors with a questioning look. She had seen Lady Jane out riding many times and she had been present at the feast at Ladsill Hall that marked the betrothal of Lady Jane and Sir Edward. Why was such a great lady in this lowly barn? The girl tried to struggle to her feet but Jane bid her stay where she was.

'I need to ask you some questions if you are strong enough to answer,' Jane began, looking searchingly at the girl. 'Firstly, is your father the landlord of The Peacock?' Jane, asked, needing to be sure she had the right girl.

Mary nodded, with downcast eyes.

'You left there some time last year did you not?' Jane questioned, listening hard for Mary's quiet reply.

'I did,' she muttered.

'And where did you go to?' Jane persisted.

''Tis no business of yours,' Mary cried, glaring at Jane.

'I think it is,' Jane stated calmly.

'What's it to you anyway?' Mary asked moodily.

'Answer my question then I will tell you.'

'I went off wi' a gentleman.'

'Does this gentleman have a name?' Jane asked patiently.

'Maybe he does and maybe he

166

doesn't,' Mary said with a certain detachment.

'Less of your cheek, miss,' Bess said angrily. 'Do you know who this is?'

'Aye, I've seen you two out riding, but you've never noticed me. He did though. He noticed me. He was kind to me at first. He carried me off to his great big house and I was important. I could have been a great lady there. No-one knew me there. He said I could be a great lady. He were going to make me into a great lady until this happened, then he threw me out.'

Mary lowered her head as if the memories were too painful. Jane shuffled uncomfortably.

'Just answer my question, Mary, then we will leave you,' Jane said, feeling rather awkward. 'Do you know Master John Fornton?'

'I'll say I do,' she answered with renewed interest. 'If it were not for him I wouldn't be here now.'

Jane felt herself go faint and Bess stepped forward to support her. She had just had her worst fears confirmed. With a last helpless look at Mary and her tiny babe, Jane left the barn leaning heavily on Bess's arm.

'Tell Syd Dawson to return to Migfield Manor and inform Master John Fornton that he will not be welcome at Ladsill ever again,' Jane sobbed as they rode away. 'I have no desire to know of his health. I do not wish to speak to him. I have no wish to hear his name ever, ever again.'

7

That night, Jane hardly slept, through the empty hours looking out over the silent countryside towards Migfield Manor. She was unaware of time, only the rage of grief and disappointment roaring through her head. Periodically she searched her mind for pity for John Fornton who had been dreadfully hurt at the hands of those ruffians, then the picture of Mary Armstrong and the tiny babe filled her mind and her grief was all for herself again. Eventually she cried herself to sleep.

With the first light of a cool, grey dawn she was awake again, aware even before her mind cleared of sleep of a dreadful aching emptiness inside her. She lay still, her mind roaming with resigned sadness over the happenings of the previous day. Bess entered the chamber a while later and her morning greeting died on her lips as she saw her mistress's opaque eyes. She looked flustered as she hurried forward, thrusting unruly strands of her frizzled grey hair under her cap.

'Did you not sleep well?' she enquired taking Jane's hand in hers and looking questioningly into her eyes.

'I fear I didn't, Bess, and when I slept I saw images of John and Mary with her baby. I don't wish the girl harm, but my feelings towards her are far from charitable.'

'That's understandable. I wanted to box her ears, but that wouldn't have helped either, would it!'

A giant smile touched Jane's lips but failed to reach her eyes as Bess busied herself arranging her mistress's clothes.

'You'd better make haste now, your father is asking for you. He wants you to join him in his study promptly.'

It was only later when she stood before her father that Jane gave any thought to the pending visit of Sir Edward.

'Sit down, Jane,' her father said indicating a stool while he himself continued to pace the floor. 'I have just received a message informing me that Lady Sutton has died. As you will shortly be the next Lady Sutton it would seem appropriate that I should attend this funeral. Naturally if you should wish to accompany me in order to express your personal condolences to Sir Edward I would be delighted to have your company.'

'Could I be excused, Father? You will be able to convey the feelings I had towards Lady Sutton in a much more appropriate manner.'

The edge of Sir George's mouth twitched as he recalled the lack of harmony between the two ladies at Christmas. He bent forward and placed a kiss on his daughter's head.

'I must leave immediately but I want you to be prepared now, Jane. I think with the death of Lady Sutton, Sir Edward will understandably be wanting to hurry your wedding forward.'

'You mean now he doesn't simply want a wife, he wants a replacement for his mother, to keep his houses in order!'

Sir George's dark brows drew together yet he made no reply as he collected up some papers and wished her good-day. A few days ago, she would have argued, begged him to call off the marriage, but now she simply didn't care. She would have to marry someone so why not Sir Edward? Once she had done her wifely duty of bearing him a son, she was quite sure he would leave her alone and seek his pleasures elsewhere.

In a daze, Jane wandered out into the hall where Bess was waiting. Quickly and quietly, she relayed the information and Bess's wrinkled face sobered as she looked at her intently.

It saddened her to see her sweet mistress made to suffer so.

For four days the weather was unpredictable then the fifth day dawned with all the transient beauty of March with an arch of sky as clear and blue as

172

summer. Bess suggested a ride and as they set off, Jane found it easier to relax as they rode through the fields and into the woods where many of the trees blushed with a faint hint of green in readiness for the new season.

A fast gallop over the moors brought them on to the highway running away towards Lectonfield. They checked their pace as a single rider galloped towards them and both ladies were surprised and apprehensive to discover the rider was John Fornton. His beaming smile of welcome was warm and sincere yet it met only cold looks.

'My dearest Jane,' he said removing his cap and giving a deep bow. 'This is an unexpected pleasure. Do you have business in this direction?'

She made no effort to offer her hand in greeting as she replied sharply, 'No, sir, we are simply taking the air.'

'Then would you allow me to escort you back to Ladsill Hall? I was on my way to see your father.'

'Then I can save you the trouble,

Master Fornton. My father is not at home.'

'In that case, may I escort you anyway? It isn't often that I get the opportunity to ride with such pleasant company.'

'Pleasant company has caused many men to go astray, has it not, Master Fornton?'

John looked at her questioningly yet her words were lost on him. He turned to Bess who simply shrugged her shoulders and raised quizzical brows.

'Am I supposed to place some meaning in that statement?' John asked moving his horse round to enable him to look fully at Jane.

'I merely stated that you, like many young men, find the pleasant company of pretty girls highly desirable, Master Fornton. Do you not?'

John looked at her in puzzlement.

'Since I laid eyes on you I have had no wish to look at another. You are the only face that I crave to see and my heart belongs to you and only you.'

'Pretty words, Master Fornton, and you say them so easily, yet not ten miles from here lies a girl with a pretty face and a new-born child — your child, I believe.'

John gave a confused laugh.

'My child?' he asked in bewilderment. 'On whose word do you accept that I have a child?'

'The girl herself.'

'Then she has lied. I repeat, I have no interest in any other woman. Since I met you, you have occupied my every thought. How could I even look at another when my eyes would only compare her disfavourably.'

'More pretty words, Master Fornton, yet I have the word of Mary Armstrong and she says to the contrary.'

'Mary Armstrong?' John asked, mentally juggling with the situation. 'You think that I . . . that the baby . . . Oh, my darling girl, you are so very wrong. Come, and if you will escort me, together we will confront Mary Armstrong.'

'No, sir, it would not be proper,' Jane cried in alarm.

'Then how else will you know the truth? Perhaps if Bess could be persuaded to be the judge and act as witness,' John suggested.

Bess nodded her agreement, reasoning that Jane was simply carrying out a responsibility as her mother would have done, taking an interest in the welfare of a poor, unmarried mother and her child. This finally persuaded Jane and they set off to the woodsman's cottage. In the yard, John reigned in his horse, dismounted and helped the two ladies dismount. Jane held herself rigid and aloof and, without a word of thanks, entered the stable where Mary showed surprise and embarrassment as she bobbed a curtsey.

'You are looking much stronger,' Jane said with a pallid smile.

'Aye, I am, thank you, ma'am. I'm getting good food and he's a fine, strong baby.'

Jane glanced across at the sleeping babe.

'Have you given him a name?'

'John.'

'After his father.'

'No.' Mary laughed. 'After John Fornton.'

'But I thought you said . . . ' Jane stopped in confusion. 'Is John Fornton not his father?'

'Nay. Master Fornton wouldn't look at the likes o' me. He's a gentleman. He helped me when I were lying by the wayside, waiting and 'oping to die. Father wouldn't allow me through the door and nobody else wanted to know neither.'

Mary gave a sniff as she continued.

'I 'ad no shelter and Master Fornton arranged for me to come 'ere. I 'adn't eaten for days and 'e arranged for me to be fed. And when the baby was born, 'e arranged for help. He were considerate and kind and I want my baby to grow up with them qualities. I can't give 'im 'is father's name, so I gave him the name John to live up to.'

Jane felt very humble. She had

obviously misunderstood and mis-judged John and a warm, loving feeling crept into her heart. There was just one more thing she needed to know and taking a deep breath, she asked, 'Who is the father of this child, and why will he take no responsibility? You said he was a gentleman and you had been to his home. Surely his doors would not be closed against his own son.'

'Lady Jane,' Mary said with a weak smile, 'your world and mine are very different and I know my place. A gentleman would want nothing to do wi' the like o' me except for one thing, then they cast us aside. A son born out of wedlock is no proud achievement. Oh, yes, 'e might pay me off to stay away, but I 'aven't got the energy to walk back to Lancashire to 'ave the doors slammed in me face.'

'Lancashire?' Jane repeated, a sicken-ing feeling beginning to turn in her stomach.

Before Mary said another word she knew that the father was Sir Edward

Sutton but she had to be sure this time. No room for confusion of wrong notions now.

'Aye,' Mary continued. ''Tis a long way to Lancashire. My lord 'as a castle there built like a fortress with a moat round. I used to walk along the leaded roof and look at the view for miles.'

She stopped, remembering as she pictured the landscape in her mind's eye.

'Later, when he'd given me a bad time, I used to walk along the roof and look down into the moat thinking how easy it would be to jump and end it all. Then I concocted a plot to get him up there, and push him over the edge. He deserves to die. He's a wicked man. Trouble was, he threw me out afore I could.'

Jane looked from the distraught Mary to Bess who sat motionless on a pile of straw. Try as she might, she could not bring herself to voice his name, but taking a deep breath she asked, 'Do I know him, this tyrant?'

'Aye, Lady Jane,' she muttered almost inaudibly. 'He stayed at The Peacock afore you announced your betrothal but even that night he took me to his bed.'

Her voice trailed off and she dropped her eyes in embarrassment.

'You mean the child is Sir Edward's?' Jane asked, her voice almost a whisper.

Mary nodded her head without raising her eyes. Jane felt hurt and humiliated yet strangely elated. There was now no mistake. Mary had told her more than she had bargained for. The silence was broken by a sob and Jane's gaze darted across to Mary.

'I'm so sorry, miss,' she choked between the sobs. 'Now you know. This innocent babe here is the son of your intended lord and I'm no better than a common slut.'

Jane looked at the girl with pity.

'Why did you do it?' she questioned gently.

Mary screwed up her nose, gave a few deep sniffs and stopped sobbing as she ran her arm over her eyes and nose.

'You wouldn't understand, my lady.'

'Try me!'

Mary gave another deep sniff.

'There's always work from daybreak to dusk and even then there's sewing and spinning and mending. Then Sir Edward started to call regularly and he'd sit wi' me and tell me nice tales. I thought, why can't I be rich and live in a castle like Ladsill Hall, and wear fine clothes and never 'ave to scrub and clean and darn clothes again?'

Mary paused, shooting a quick glance at Jane whose face remained impassive.

'Well,' Mary continued, 'after that first night, every time he came to Ladsill, he came to me until he began to get worried that you might find out, so he took me to his castle in Lancashire. I didn't mean to hurt you, my lady,' Mary stated, a pleading expression in her eyes.

'You have not hurt me, Mary,' Jane assured her with a deep sigh. 'But I must ask you a favour.'

'Anything, miss,' Mary replied instantly.

'I want you tell my father all you have just told me.'

'Oh, I couldn't, my lady. Please don't ask me. I just couldn't. He would 'ave me horse-whipped within an inch of me life. I'm no coward, but I could no more face Sir George than jump off that roof into Sir Edward's moat.'

'But, Mary,' Jane pleaded, 'this is very important to me and my father must know the truth. Possibly if I told you you had done me a great favour, would that help?'

'Done you a favour, my lady?' Mary asked between sobs. 'I don't understand.'

'My father thinks Sir Edward is upright and just and a perfect partner for me. I know Sir Edward to be cruel and wicked and the thought of being married to him is utterly repulsive to me. I need to convince my father that this marriage must be called off so that

I can marry the man of my choosing.'

'But, my lady, I can't face your father and tell him all this.'

'No, but I can,' came a voice from the doorway and all eyes turned to see John Fornton standing there.

'I'm sorry,' he said striding into the barn. 'I couldn't bear the waiting.'

He walked over to Jane and, taking her hands in his, gazed into her eyes questioningly.

'Are you all right, my love?' he whispered, the concern in his eyes mirrored in his voice.

'Yes, my lord,' she mumbled looking anxiously into his face. 'Mary has told me everything, including the fact that Sir Edward is the baby's father. Will you forgive me for doubting you?'

Before John could reply, baby John began to cry loudly and Jane gave an embarrassed laugh.

'I'm sorry we've woken the baby with all this talk. Come, we must leave now.'

With a smile and nod to Mary, Jane turned to Bess who struggled up from her seat and without hesitation they left the barn. John helped them into their saddles and escorted them back to Ladsill Hall. Sir George had returned a short while earlier and Jane and John lost no time in tracking him down in his study.

He had been sitting beside a roaring fire, his head bent in cupped hands, yet as they entered, he rose and, offering open arms to Jane, greeted his daughter tenderly. After a moment's hesitation, he took John Fornton's hand and shook it warmly.

'I dare say neither of you has heard the news,' he queried, looking first at one then the other.

Their questioning expressions confirmed they had no idea of what he spoke.

'Sir Edward Sutton is dead.'

'Dead?' they echoed in unison as Sir George motioned for them to sit.

'I left immediately so as to impart the news personally.'

'How did he die, Father?' Jane

questioned almost unwilling to accept such welcome news for fear it was a mistake.

Sir George leaned back in his chair watching them both with interest.

'Several weeks ago, the uncle of Sir Ralph Bandale who blamed Sir Edward for his nephew's untimely death, challenged him to a duel. Sir Edward was wounded in the fight but as he didn't want word of this to get out, he accepted the unskilled treatment of a barber surgeon. Instead of getting better, the wounds never properly healed and, mounting his horse to attend his mother's funeral, he slipped and opened up the wounds afresh. When the surgeon saw him it was too late. Within two days he was dead. I am so sorry, my child,' he said with feeling, leaning over and taking Jane's hand between his.

'Father, I feel no sorrow for the passing of Sir Edward. He was a fiend and a brute. I feel no sadness, only a blessed release from a most odious duty.'

'I grant you, my daughter, he was not the man I thought him to be. His father was a gentleman yet Sir Edward bore no resemblance to him at all. I did not know that when I arranged your marriage. How could I know that he was Satan himself?'

With a long, lingering look at his daughter, Sir George turned to John Fornton.

'Rumour has it that you have recently received severe punishment at the hands of Sir Edward's henchmen, Master Fornton. I hope you are now well recovered.'

'Indeed, I am, Sir George. My recuperation will be all the quicker now with your welcome news.'

'My children, it is my duty to inform numerous people about the death of Sir Edward, so if you will excuse me. We will meet later at dinner, Master Fornton. The hospitality of Ladsill is at your disposal for as long as you wish to stay.'

Jane stared at her father in pleasant

surprise, then, bobbing a curtsey, left the room followed by John.

'Lady Jane, will you walk with me and point out all the interesting features of the view before the light is too dim?' John asked bowing to Jane.

'Master Fornton, I would love to,' Jane said placing her hand lightly on John's offered arm.

As they walked they spoke easily together until John stopped abruptly and gazed across the landscape. Jane paused and watched him with interest as he slowly turned to face her. There was a magnetism that slowly drew them together until she could feel the beating of his heart. His arms went round her and she rested hers lightly on his broad chest.

'You know why we have stopped here?' he asked lightly.

She shook her head slowly and tried to sound mystified as she gave him a bashful glance from beneath her long lashes and replied, 'I have no idea.'

'This is exactly the spot I held you in

my arms once before.'

'And you said it was an error. Are you going to make the same error again, Master Fornton?' she asked innocently, her smile teasing him.

He lifted one hand and with long, lean fingers traced the contours of her face letting them slide slowly down to her pert, little chin which he cupped and lifted to within inches of his own. He looked deeply into her eyes, seeing the flames flicker in their depths as she returned his gaze. For a moment, time stood still.

'I love you,' he whispered, his lips almost stroking hers. 'I love you more than life itself.'

'I love you,' she breathed, feeling the heat from his lips then welcoming their light pressure on hers.

He looked down at her with such love she gave a sudden little laugh.

'Did that really happen?' she asked mischievously.

He gave her a questioning look yet made no attempt to release her from his arms.

'Do you find it as regrettable as you did that first time?' she teased. 'Do you beg for my forgiveness?' she taunted him with an impish laugh.

He pulled her to him, tightening his grip of her slender frame.

'How can you taunt me when you know that the first kiss was the most wonderful thing that could happen? I kissed you then because I could not help myself. The realisation of what I had done made me ashamed of my impulses, but not my actions. You were betrothed to another and that made you another man's property.'

'That is no longer the case, my lord. I am a free person and can choose the man I wish to marry.'

'Then I will have to make sure that you make a wise choice.'

'Indeed you will, Master Fornton. Whom would you suggest I choose?'

John pretended to give the matter considerable thought before replying, 'I may be biased, but have you considered me?'

'Yes,' she replied.

'And?'

'You have not asked me.'

John released her and sank down on one knee before her. He took her hand and kissed it lightly before looking up into her face with an honest, open longing that made her go weak at the knees.

'Jane, will you do me the honour of becoming my wife?' he asked with sincerity.

'I would be delighted,' she replied with a look that mirrored his love.

In one instant she was back in his arms and his mouth claimed hers as her arms folded round the broadness of his shoulders.

'I love you,' he said when eventually he raised his head. 'I am the most fortunate man alive and I thank God that you will at last be mine.'

'My darling, wonderful John, before we make plans should you not ask my father's permission for my hand in marriage?'

'Later,' he said against her lips. 'I just want this moment to last a little longer.'

His lips were on hers again and they were lost in oblivion as the evening colours faded and nature drew the curtain of nightfall across the sky.

THE END

We do hope that you have enjoyed reading this large print book.

Did you know that all of our titles are available for purchase?

We publish a wide range of high quality large print books including:
Romances, Mysteries, Classics
General Fiction
Non Fiction and Westerns

Special interest titles available in large print are:
The Little Oxford Dictionary
Music Book, Song Book
Hymn Book, Service Book

Also available from us courtesy of Oxford University Press:
Young Readers' Dictionary
(large print edition)
Young Readers' Thesaurus
(large print edition)

For further information or a free brochure, please contact us at:
Ulverscroft Large Print Books Ltd.,
The Green, Bradgate Road, Anstey,
Leicester, LE7 7FU, England.
Tel: (00 44) 0116 236 4325
Fax: (00 44) 0116 234 0205

VISIONS OF THE HEART

Christine Briscomb

When property developer Connor Grant contracted Natalie Jensen to landscape the grounds of his large country house near Ashley in South Australia, she was ecstatic. But then she discovered he was acquiring — and ripping apart — great swathes of the town. Her own mother's house and the hall where the drama group met were two of his targets. Natalie was desperate to stop Connor's plans — but she also had to fight the powerful attraction flowing between them.

FINGALA, MAID OF RATHAY

Mary Cummins

On his deathbed, Sir James Montgomery of Rathay asks his daughter, Fingala, to swear that she will not honour her marriage contract until her brother Patrick, the new heir, returns from serving the King. Patrick must marry. Rathay must not be left without a mistress. But Patrick has fallen in love with the Lady Catherine Gordon whom the King, James IV, has given in marriage to the young man who claims to be Richard of York, one of the princes in the Tower.